THE
DARK UNICORN

PRAISE FOR THE DARK UNICORN

"Cptivates the interest of the reader from the beginning . . . the action moves quickly, holding your interest until the end."

— SASKATCHEWAN BOOK AWARDS
JUDGES

THE DARK UNICORN

EDWARD WILLETT

THE DARK UNICORN

Published by
Endless Sky Books
Regina, Saskatchewan, Canada
endless-sky-books.com

Second edition
First edition published 1998 by Royal Fireworks Press
This edition copyright © 2025 by Edward Willett
All rights reserved

Print ISBN: 978-1-989398-95-1
Ebook ISBN: 978-1-989398-96-8

For Wendi, who inspired it

CONTENTS

CHAPTER I

THE STRANGER ON THE BRIDGE

The actors on the rickety wooden stage had almost finished their bawdy skit. Master Kilrik raised his baton, and Nels hastily pulled his frozen fingers out of his armpits and snatched up the flute from his lap. "Together, this time!" Kilrik snapped. His pudgy, round face glowed red with the cold, as did the bald spot on the back of his head when he glanced over his shoulder at the stage.

The actors bowed, the score or so of people huddled in the Dancing Swan's run-down courtyard pattered barely polite applause, and Kilrik gave the downbeat.

Nels played mechanically, his fingers so stiff with cold that he found it hard to keep them moving at the tempo of the silly bouncy tune that closed every performance. But he'd played that tune so many times he no longer had to think about it. Instead, his thoughts drifted back to the letter he'd received from his mother that morning—until he suddenly found himself playing a solo, which ended with an unmusical squeak. Kilrik must have been cold, too; he'd cut off an entire chorus.

Not looking at the musicmaster, but very much aware of his glare, Nels hastily dismantled his flute and tucked it into its padded wooden case as the other four musicians hurried away. He got up to follow, but of course, it wasn't going to be that easy.

"I thought you told Strom you were a musician," Kilrik said, his sarcasm more biting than the wind.

Nels kept his eyes down. "I am a musician, Master Kilrik."

Kilrik prodded him in the chest with the tip of his baton. "Musicians keep their minds on their music and their eyes on their conductors! They don't embarrass the ensemble before an audience!"

Nels glanced around the courtyard. The actors had disappeared into their warm wagons the moment they'd finished their bows, and the crowd—if that wasn't too grand a term—had dispersed into the inn and surrounding houses seconds later. They'd been playing for no one but themselves.

Nels knew better than to point that out to Kilrik, though. "I'm sorry, Master."

"And just what *were* you thinking of?"

"A letter from home, Master." The instant he'd said it, Nels regretted it—but the damage was done.

"From your mother, no doubt. Didn't you say she taught you to play the flute? Perhaps that's why you play so badly!"

Nels clenched his fists.

But Kilrik kept on. "Well, boy, this isn't three drunken fishermen banging spoons together. This is a professional ensemble, and I run it. I won't have anyone in it who isn't pulling his weight. Do I make myself clear?"

Nels had made the mistake once of telling Kilrik what he thought of his "professional" ensemble, whose other members were an arthritic harpist, blind in one eye, a drummer who couldn't tell noise from rhythm, a cornet player Nels had yet to see sober, and a tone-deaf fiddler. Now he knew better. Kilrik had never forgiven him, especially since their employer, Strom, had overheard him and laughed uproariously. "Maybe I should make *him* music-master, Kilrik!" he'd shouted.

Since then, Kilrik had taken every opportunity to make Nels's life miserable—and had succeeded admirably. He nodded submissively and turned to go.

But Kilrik still wasn't finished. "And when you write back to your fishwife mother, tell her someday I hope to be able to teach you how a flute is really played!"

Nels spun and leaped at him. Kilrik yelped as they crashed to the ground and cowered beneath Nels's pummelling fists, yelling for help.

Strom shouted from his wagon, and Nels suddenly realized what he was doing and jumped up, stumbling back from the fallen musicmaster. Kilrik whimpered, hands covering his face and blood oozing out between his fingers: that must have been his nose Nels had felt squish so delightfully.

Strom shouted again, and the door to his wagon opened. Nels grabbed the flute case from his stool and clattered across the courtyard's cobblestones and out the open gate.

He skidded to a halt in the street, looked frantically right and left, then heard Strom's voice again, furious now, and dashed right, plunging into the first alley he came to and then doing his best to lose himself in the twisting, narrow lanes of Nimgar.

He succeeded only too well; as full darkness descended on the city an hour later, he was still wandering aimlessly, not knowing how to even begin to make his way back to the Dancing Swan.

And he would have to go back, he knew; running away had only made things worse. His back itched as he thought of facing Strom after having attacked the music-master. Not that Strom had any great affection for Kilrik; far from it. But Strom did have great affection for what he called discipline, dispensed with a whip.

Yet, Nels had nowhere else to go. Home was a hundred miles away, and the letter from his mother had made it clear he couldn't go back there.

He stopped in the flickering light of a lone torch at the corner of two otherwise pitch-black streets, sat down with his back against the blackened bricks of a boarded-up building, and opened his flute case. From a pocket in the padded lining, he drew out the bit of parchment the travelling peddler had delivered that morning, and read it again, imagining his mother's musical voice . . .

My dearest son.

I hope you are well and happy in the new life you have chosen. I know that you love music; it must be wonderful to be able to perform with others who feel the same way.

Nels thought bitterly of Kilrik and the drunken horn player.

We are all well, but we miss you deeply. However, I feel perhaps the One has guided you well, for we are hard-pressed to feed and clothe your younger brothers and sisters. Your older brothers are, of course, helping your father fish, but we really need another boat, and we cannot afford to have one built. Pinna and Kars have talked of building one themselves, but it would take them many weeks, and then who would help your father? And worse, the catches have been very poor this year. Your father is very worried; he says the fish have all fled north.

Rika is of an age to marry, but Gull Rock is so small that there are no eligible men. She is a comfort to me, however, and works hard; she is now teaching Lila, Biki and Miki to read, and I am teaching Tami, Tisha, and Hanissa music.

I have faith the fishing will recover; I'm sure everything will yet be all right. In the meantime, I am thankful that you, at least, have found a place in the world where you can do what you most want. I pray to the One daily for your safety. Your father sends his love, as do your brothers and sisters. I know it is difficult to find travellers who will come as far out of their way as Gull Rock, but you would make my heart glad if you were to write.

With utmost love, Mama

Nels swallowed hard. He swiped his woollen sleeve across his eyes, then carefully folded the letter and put it back in the flute case.

"I have to get some money back to them," he whispered. But how? His allowance from Strom was so meagre that he'd saved only a few coppers, and he needed new boots before the winter closed in.

He'd have to ask Strom for more. His back twitched again at the thought. To think he had once liked, even admired, the man!

Nels had been one of just a handful of people, mostly children and women, who had come out to see the troupe when it had passed through Gull Rock more than a year ago; there might have been more, but on such a fine day, fishermen had better things to do than idle away hours watching a play.

The actors performed *The Wizard Wacundra and the Great Gondwain*, a tale of a thousand years ago, when legend said magic still lived in the Heartland. In the play, Gondwain, with Wacundra's help, drove back the evil hordes of the Blood Empire, but used up all the magic in the Heartland doing it, which nicely explained why there wasn't any around anymore.

Having seen the play a hundred more times since joining Strom's troupe, Nels could barely remember how he had felt that first night, as monsters and demons and warriors came to life and battled before his very eyes. He'd longed to *be* Gondwain the Great. He remembered looking south, where the Wall was a mile-high black curtain in the sky, thrilled to think that he had just seen Gondwain create it.

At fourteen, Nels had already known all too well how hard-pressed his parents were to support their large family, and had known, too, that the life of a fisherman was not for him. Pinna and Kars, his older brothers, loved the sea, but Nels found far more interest in his father's tales of far-off parts of the Heartland, where his father had soldiered in the king's service during the Desolation Rebellion, or the things his mother had learned during her days as a servant of a minor noble, before a dashing young soldier swept her off her feet and took her home with him to Gull Rock.

One of the things his mother had learned had been to play the flute; to play it so beautifully that when she left the noble's service, he gave her a beautiful silver flute as a wedding gift. In Nels, she found an avid student, and on his tenth birthday, she passed the flute on to him. After that, there were many days when he should have been helping his brothers mend nets or sails that he'd spent instead seated on the towering stone cliff that gave Gull Rock its name, playing a piping counterpoint to the piercing cries of the seabirds and the bass-drum rumble of the surf below.

Strom's troupe seemed like a door to him, a door to a

larger world, a door that might close and never reopen if he didn't seize his chance to go through it. That night, he left a note for his parents on the table by his bed, then sneaked out of the house through the window of the room he shared with his brothers and set off through the darkness along the road to Petra, the troupe's next destination.

He'd found the troupe the next morning and recognized Strom at once, though out of make-up, the burly, bushy-haired giant now harnessing a horse to his wagon would not have been anyone's vision of the great hero Gondwain.

Still glowing with his memory of the play, Nels went straight up to him. "I want to come with you."

Strom didn't stop tightening cinches. "Do you, now?

"Very much."

Strom gave the leather a final tug and leaned his back against the huge horse, which flicked an ear but otherwise ignored him. "And why should I want you?"

"I can play the flute."

"Let's hear you, then."

Fingers trembling, Nels set the flute case on the ground, drew out the instrument, and fitted it together. Afterward, he could never remember what he played, but apparently it did the trick: after a couple of minutes, Strom waved his hand. "That'll do. All right, boy. Happens we could use another musician . . . but you'll have to do more than that."

"Anything, sir!"

"I also need someone to keep my wagon clean and look after my horse. Can you handle that?"

"Yes, sir!"

"Then climb in the back. We've a long day ahead."

For a week, Nels had enjoyed the time with the troupe as much as he'd thought he would; Strom made him work hard but seemed affable enough, and Nels had not yet played enough with Kilrik's "orchestra" to recognize its (and Kilrik's) incompetence.

But at the end of the week, the troupe stopped in a village fifty miles up the coast from Gull Rock, a village with, as Strom himself put it, the personality of a pickle. Few people came to see them; fewer still paid.

Around midnight, the door to Strom's wagon crashed open, jolting Nels from deep sleep on his pallet at the back. Strom stormed in, bringing with him a strong smell of sour wine. Nels, heart pounding, lay perfectly still as Strom rummaged around in the chest under his bed for a few minutes, then suddenly swore and strode over to Nels. He grabbed Nels's arm with meaty, vice-like fingers and snarled into his face, "I had a bottle of brandy in my chest, boy. Where is it?"

Nels almost gagged. Whatever vintage Strom had been imbibing, its stale bouquet didn't go well with the garlic sausage and onions Strom must have had for supper. "I—I don't know, sir!"

"Liar!" Strom threw him to the floor and reached for the horsewhip hanging over his bed. "I'll teach you!"

The whip descended, hissing, and Nels suddenly

jerked awake, staring around at the darkened streets for a moment in complete confusion, still lost in the memory that had somehow become a dream. He wiped icy sweat from his face with a shaky hand, then got up and started walking again, knowing it was only too likely the dream would become reality when he returned to the Dancing Swan.

He had moved out of Strom's wagon the next day, but he still had to keep it clean, and any time Strom had been drinking and found the slightest thing out of order—and sometimes even when he didn't—Nels could expect a beating. His back was scarred from repeated "lessons," and he wondered if Strom had ever been a slavemaster. He grimaced. "He's a slavemaster now," he muttered.

He smelled a sour, gassy stench, and a moment later emerged from the alley onto the bank of the river, which slid by dark and oily in the starlight. At once, Nels regained his bearings. Somewhere off to his left had to be the bridge they'd crossed on their way to the inn; once on that road, he knew he could find his way back.

He walked slowly along the bank, listening to the gurgle of the sewage-fouled water and thinking of the clean waves of the ocean pounding against the Gull Rock cliffs. Suddenly, light flared on the far bank. A man shouted hoarsely; another answered—then the light vanished.

Nels stared at the spot where it had been. Strom, searching for him? Surely not, not on that side of the river. "Nothing to do with me," he murmured.

He walked on and, all too soon, reached the bridge. There he paused, gazing up at the stars. At least they were the same here as at home.

Footsteps pounded across the bridge toward him, uneven, stumbling. Out of the darkness loomed a man, panting for breath. He crashed into Nels, who grabbed him instinctively, and felt something warm and sticky on the man's back. "You're bleeding!"

"Crossbow bolt . . . went right through." The man coughed, then drew a bubbling breath. "Help me, hide me!"

"What?"

"For the One's sake, you've got to—to—" He choked, and sagged to his knees.

"I'll go get help," Nels said desperately. "The city guard . . ."

"No time!" The stranger reached up and pulled Nels down to him with surprising strength. Even in the darkness, Nels could see dark blood dripping from his mouth. "Take this, take it and run!" He jerked something from a string around his neck and thrust it into Nels's hand: a leather pouch with something hard and angular inside.

"But what . . ."

"He must have crossed the bridge!" someone suddenly cried. "There's blood on the stones!"

"Run!" the wounded man pleaded. "Keep that safe. Someone will come for it. Now go!" A spasm gripped him, and he doubled over, choking.

"But . . ."

Footsteps clattered on the bridge, and Nels gave up arguing and fled, wondering as he did so if he shouldn't have stayed behind, tried to help the hurt man . . .

But then he heard a gurgling scream behind him, cut short, and knew it was too late. Whoever had been chasing the man had found him.

Nels wondered how long it would be before they found *him*.

CHAPTER 2
SHADOW'S VANISHING ACT

Back on the main road, with terror at his heels and the murdered man's dying gift burning a hole in his shirt pocket, Nels reached the Dancing Swan in minutes. Finding the courtyard gate locked for the night, he ran instead to the front door. He burst through it and slammed it shut behind him, then leaned against its rough wood, gasping, as curious customers looked up from their ale.

He'd hoped to slip unobserved to his wagon, but as he straightened, his eyes met those of Strom, already rising from a table by the fire he shared with Kilrik.

For a wild moment, Nels considered dashing out into the street again, but Strom had already reached him. "Let's have words, boy," the troupe leader growled, grabbing Nels's arm in one ham-like hand. The smell of wine and something stronger hung around him, and a bit of Nels deep inside retreated like a turtle pulling its legs and head into its shell. Though the dying scream of the man at the bridge had propelled him back to the inn with the thought of telling Strom what had happened, that idea vanished in the harsh reality of the casual brutality with which Strom jerked him across the inn floor, pushing lesser men out of the way.

Strom dragged him across the cobblestones to his wagon and shoved him inside, then took down the horse-whip from its all-too-familiar place. "Kilrik is the master and you are the apprentice," he slurred. "Maybe this will help you remember!" The whip descended.

When at last Strom pushed Nels outside again and strode back toward the yellow light and loud voices of the common room, Nels crouched on the cold stones for a moment on his hands and knees. The whip had momen-tarily driven the dying man at the bridge from his mind, but as the pain eased to a familiar burning and throbbing, he remembered, and scrambled up and scuttled to his wagon like a startled rabbit.

He leaped the three steps to the door and crashed through, slamming it behind him. Then he gasped as light flared in the darkness. Elongated black eyes in a thin brown face met his.

If he'd shared his wagon with anyone but Shadow, Nels might have asked for help. But Shadow was the strangest of all their motley troupe.

He wore only black: black tunic, black trousers, and black cloak, as black as his short-cropped hair and his eyes. The grey that sprinkled his neatly trimmed black beard only accentuated the darkness of the rest of him.

He rarely spoke, and he said nothing now, lying on his bed and watching in silence as Nels took a deep breath and began undoing the buttons of his shirt. But as he removed it, Shadow asked softly, "Strom?"

"I guess he didn't like me knocking down his music-master." Nels tossed the shirt on the thinly padded shelf that served as his bed, then opened one of the drawers under the shelf and took out a small clay pot. He sat down on the bed, dipped his fingers in the sweet-smelling pale cream it contained and tried to apply it to his burning back, but his bruised muscles were stiffening, and he couldn't reach the lash marks.

"Let me." Shadow swung his feet off his bed and crossed the wagon, holding out his hand for the vial of cream. Astonished, Nels gave it to him. Shadow picked up Nels's discarded, bloody shirt, held it for a moment, then put it to one side before sitting down on the bed beside Nels. He dipped his fingers in the salve and began spreading it on Nels's back. The thick paste took the fire from the stripes, reducing the pain to a throb.

"Why did you knock down Kilrik?" Shadow asked as he worked.

"He's incompetent."

"If everyone met incompetence with violence, most of this troupe would have long since been killed by audiences."

"And he insulted my mother."

"Ah." Silence for a moment, but Shadow had already spoken as many words as Nels had ever heard him string together at one time. And, amazingly, he wasn't done yet. "What happened after you ran off?"

Nels stiffened. Why did he want to know? What did he *already* know? "I wandered around for a while, then came back. That's all."

"Oh?" Shadow reached for Nels's shirt and, before Nels could react, pulled from its pocket the leather pouch the dying man had given him. "And what's this?"

Nels lunged for it, but Shadow snatched it back. As Nels stared, he raised it to his forehead, eyes closed, then dropped it as if it were hot. "I was not mistaken," he cried. "Take it back!"

As Nels clenched it protectively in his fist, Shadow backed away from him until he stood at the far end of the wagon, the vial of ointment forgotten in one hand.

Nels stared at him. "You know what happened, don't you?"

"I told them!" Shadow whispered, staring at the fist that held the pouch. "They thought I was mad. But I *knew* I sensed it moving!"

Nels slowly opened his hand and looked at the pouch. "What are you talking about? What *is* this thing?"

Shadow took a deep breath. "Open it."

Warily, Nels lifted the little pouch to the level of his eyes and examined it closely. It looked harmless, but a man had already died for whatever was in it. "I should just throw it away," he muttered.

"No!" Shadow stumbled forward, hands outstretched, but stopped without touching him. "No! You must not. It's safer with you than with anyone else, because no one knows you have it. But if you throw it away, someone else may find it!"

"But what is it?"

"Open it!"

Common sense told him that if he just threw it away, if he never looked inside it, nobody could accuse him of stealing it, or come looking for it later. But common sense was no match for curiosity, not just about the pouch's contents but Shadow's strange intensity.

With his index finger, Nels tentatively tugged at the pouch's mouth. It opened easily, and he turned the bag upside down over his open hand.

Into his palm dropped the tiny black figure of a rearing unicorn, no more than an inch tall, delicately carved out of some substance that reflected nothing of the lamplight, though it felt glassy-smooth to Nels's touch.

A fine silver chain was strung through a loop attached to the unicorn's back.

Shadow stepped forward, eyes wide. "A unicorn! That explains many mysteries . . ."

"Not to me!" Nels growled. "What's so special about this thing?"

But abruptly, Shadow stiffened and backed away again. "It's not safe for you to know anything more about it. I've already said more than I should."

"But how did you know I had it?"

"No more questions." Shadow pulled his cloak from the peg at the foot of his bed and slung it around his shoulders.

A horrible thought occurred to Nels. "Were you there? Were you one of those who killed the man who gave it to me?"

"I was not." He sat down on his bed and pulled on his boots.

"Where are you going?"

Shadow stood and stamped each boot heel in turn. "I have pressing business elsewhere." He started toward the door.

Nels jumped up and grabbed his arm. "Not until you tell me what's going on!"

Shadow pulled his arm free with surprising strength and shoved Nels sharply in the chest, sending him stumbling back to his bed. "I have interfered too much already! Keep the unicorn hidden, and keep it safe. Someone will come for it." He slipped out, the door banging shut behind him.

"That's what I'm afraid of," Nels muttered. He started to lie on his back, then jerked upright, swearing, and lay on his side instead.

It took him a long time to fall asleep, and the instant he finally did, it seemed shouts and the clatter of hooves on cobblestones woke him. Someone knocked on the door, then threw it open before he could do more than sit up, blinking in the sudden flood of daylight and frosty air. A bearded face stared at Shadow's empty bed. "Where'd he get to?" Axon, the stagemaster, demanded. "He should have been helping me pack for the last half-hour."

I wish I knew, Nels thought. "I don't know. He left in the middle of the night . . ."

Axon disappeared, leaving the door open. As Nels rolled stiffly out of bed, he heard the man shout, "Strom! Shadow ran out on us!"

Strom appeared as Nels slipped gingerly into his shirt. "Did Shadow say why he was leaving?" Strom boomed, his breath filling the doorway with steam.

"He said he had pressing business." Nels didn't look at the troupe leader.

"I'll bet he did." Strom glanced over his shoulder at something. "And so do we. Get this wagon ready, boy. We've worn out our welcome in Nimgar."

Snatches of conversation Nels overheard from the others in the troupe as he hitched the horses to his wagon told him what had happened, and added urgency to his task.

The man killed on the bridge had been found in the night. Nimgar was a quiet city; murders were rare, and nobody knew who the dead man was, which made the city guard's first suspects the only other strangers in town—Strom's troupe.

Shadow's disappearance hadn't helped matters: even the other members of the troupe believed he'd killed the man, and cursed him for it, not so much for the murder as for landing the rest of them in the thick of it.

Shadow must *have killed him,* Nels thought as he

worked. *How else could he have known about the unicorn?* But that didn't make sense. If Shadow had killed someone to get the unicorn, why, when he'd had it in his hand, had he given it back to Nels, and then run off?

Nels touched the hard lump of the unicorn beneath his shirt. Once more in its leather pouch, it now hung around his neck. *I should go to the guard*, he thought . . . but how could he trust them? How could he trust anyone? For all he knew, the city guard had been the ones who murdered the man on the bridge. Even if they weren't, it didn't sound like they were interested in justice—they just wanted to pin the murder on someone handy to quiet the city's residents. They'd hang him as readily as Shadow.

Shaking his head in frustration, Nels climbed up into his wagon's driver's box. Besides the seven two-person wagons like his, there were five larger ones, one for Strom, the others used to haul the stage, sets, costumes, and instruments. Nels, having risen late, was the last driver to take up his reins; the others already awaited Strom's signal to leave.

A sullen and growing crowd had watched the troupe's preparations. Now, as Strom mounted his wagon, waved to the drivers, and started his wagon rolling toward the courtyard gate, someone by the midden heap grabbed an apple core and threw it. It banged against the side of Nels's wagon.

It was like throwing a torch into a barrel of pitch. In an instant, the air was full of whatever the townspeople could get their hands on—mud, manure, garbage, rocks. A stone whizzed past Nels's left ear, and when he ducked, a ripe tomato caught him on the side of his head so hard it made his ear ring.

As he wiped juice and seeds from his eyes, he heard someone shout, "Get them!", and the whole mob surged forward.

The drivers lashed their horses frantically, and all twelve wagons dashed for the courtyard gate. Nels, slightly ahead of the pack, got through easily, but as he glanced back, he saw two of the smallest wagons crash together, one overturning and spilling its driver and contents onto the cobblestones. The driver leaped up and swung on board the next wagon that trundled by, and as the crowd descended on the spilled wagon, righteous indignation giving way to greed, the rest of the troupe made it safely out of the courtyard.

Strom set a blistering pace through Nimgar and for a mile down the road. When at last the wagons slowed, the horses were blowing, steam rising in the cold air from their nostrils, mouths, and sweating flanks.

Nels took the time to pull over and put blankets on his horses and wipe the last of the tomato from his face; when he mounted again and drove on, he brought up the rear of the caravan, which suited him fine.

He might have left Nimgar behind, but the trouble that had started there rode with him. He touched the hard lump of the unicorn again. *I sensed it moving*, Shadow had said.

Magic? Nels snorted. He didn't believe in magic. Not

anymore. Magic was nothing but illusion, like the illusion of Strom as Gondwain the Great that had propelled him into this miserable life in the first place.

Gondwain had supposedly used all the magic in the Heartland to create the Wall that rose in Gull Rock's southern sky, but Nels had heard many men say privately the Wall was only some strange natural phenomenon on the order of earthquakes or comets, and that probably the Blood Empire and Gondwain himself were only myths invented to explain it.

Lost in thought, he almost drove into the back of the stopped wagon in front of him. Reining in hurriedly, he leaned to his left to see down the line of the caravan. Strom stood by the side of the road, waving and shouting to the drivers, and Nels got stiffly down from his perch, looped the reins around the rail on the back of the wagon in front, and went to join the rest of the troupe.

Kilrik gave him a nasty look as he hobbled up, but he ignored the musicmaster and concentrated on Strom.

"All right," the troupe leader said. "You all saw the lousy audience we got in Nimgar, even before Shadow took a notion to decrease the local population. Well, I did some asking around, and I found out why. Seems King Athelras has proclaimed a festival, and everyone who can run, walk, or crawl has gone to Koroth to take it in. Which means that's our next stop. Even this bunch of no-talent scarecrows ought to be able to make some money there. And we're going to need it, since Shadow's little escapade has cost us a wagon. Any questions?" He paused for a second, but not as if he really expected a response, and, of course, there wasn't one. "Then let's move out."

Koroth! As Nels walked back to his wagon, for a moment, he forgot everything else. Koroth, the capital of the Heartland, the home of King Athelras, once even the home of Gondwain the Great, if he ever really existed. *Koroth!* It had always seemed more a dream than reality to Nels, though his father told stories of visits there during his days as a soldier, and his mother had been there often while she served the noble. In their stories, Koroth was filled with gleaming towers, silken banners, and glittering fountains. And in two days, he would see it for himself!

But then he glanced back at Nimgar. Back there were people who had killed for what he wore around his neck, and undoubtedly would do so again. And if everyone were going to Koroth, then Koroth would be the next place they'd look.

"I hope you're still able to play after Strom's little 'lesson' last night," said a familiar and unwelcome voice. Nels took a deep breath, then turned to face Kilrik, who stood with folded arms only a few feet away. "I hope it was a lesson you learned well." He smiled unpleasantly.

Nels gripped his temper with both hands. He did not want to attract Strom's attention again, not so soon after last night's "words." If Strom found out he'd been even indirectly involved in the murder that had forced the troupe to leave *and* cost it a wagon . . .

"Yes, Master," he said, eyes contritely downcast, and Kilrik laughed and walked away.

As the wagons resumed rolling, Nels looked back at Nimgar once more. Metal flashed in the sun as someone else rode out of the gate, but whoever it was moved off the road and into the field, and Nels tried to put his sudden suspicion out of his mind. *Nothing to do with me,* he thought. *Whoever killed that man at the bridge can't possibly know I have what they're looking for.* He looked forward, resolving to put Nimgar out of his mind and think instead of the wonders of Koroth.

But his mind insisted on pointing out, as the troupe started up the forested ridge that would hide Nimgar from view, that there was no way Shadow could have known he had the unicorn, either.

CHAPTER 3
ILL NEWS FROM NIMGAR

In one of the towers of Koroth of which Nels dreamed (although, being made of grey, lichen-spotted stone, it didn't exactly shine), a tall, blonde young man only a few years older than Nels impatiently followed his father and another man up dusty, long-disused stairs.

Not, Prince Rand reflected, that his impatience ever seemed to make any difference in the slow deliberations of his father, King Athelras. As for the other man . . . having spent part of every day for most of fifteen years being tutored by him, Rand knew just how unlikely it was that anything he might say or do would alter Sartan's course of action.

Well, he respected both of them for their accumulated age and wisdom, but couldn't they at least walk a little faster?

At last, on the top floor of the tower, they came to a thick wooden door. Sartan unlocked it with a rusty key he pulled from a pocket in the sleeve of his long white robe and ushered the King and the Prince into a small, windowless room. Rand glanced at the faded red upholstery on one of the six chairs that encircled a table of black wood and decided not to sit down: the cloth looked like it would crumble into nothing if he so much as breathed on it.

At least someone had swept and dusted before they arrived, and set a silver decanter of wine and three crystal goblets on the table. Sartan poured a portion of rich red liquid into each goblet and handed one to Athelras, who accepted it with a slight bow of his head. Then he proffered one to Rand.

Rand took a quick gulp, but hardly tasted it. "So here we are, safe from prying ears," he snapped, the first words any of them had spoken since beginning the climb from the King's private chambers. "Though there are other rooms below us, considerably better furnished, that are equally safe. *Now* will you tell us what is troubling you, Sartan?"

Sartan raised one bushy white eyebrow. "Impatience ill becomes a future ruler. As I'm sure I taught you."

Athelras chuckled. "Don't tease my son, old friend. Come; tell us your secret, and why it can only be told in this room."

"Very well." Sartan carefully placed his wine on the table and sat in one of the chairs. Remarkably, it survived. He folded his hands. "The situation in the south continues to worsen."

"*That's* the secret you dragged us up here to tell us?" Rand said. "We know about the latest village-burning, Sartan. We do have sources of information besides your priests, you know."

"Enough, Rand." Athelras searched Sartan's deep blue eyes. "You've learned who did it, haven't you?"

"Perhaps you should ask the Prince," Sartan said mildly. "His 'sources of information' can surely tell you . . ."

Rand bit off an angry retort. Anger didn't work with Sartan any better than impatience did.

Athelras glanced at him. "I'm certain my son is as eager to hear your news as I am, Sartan."

Sartan inclined his head. "Very well." He spread his hands. "Magic destroyed the villages . . . magic guided by the Blood Empire."

Rand snorted. *For the love of . . .* "There is no magic! And probably no Blood Empire, either."

"You always did tend to doze off during history lessons," Sartan said. "Of course, there is magic. The very Wall that separates us from the Blood Empire *is* magic— all the magic of the Heartland, formed into an impenetrable barrier by Gondwain a thousand years ago."

"Myths and hearthside tales. The Wall is a natural phenomenon, and the Blood Empire exists in the legend created to explain it. The philosopher Kelfrick has proved it."

"Kelfrick," Sartan said, "knows how to craft words so they will capture the imagination of young nobles, but that is all he knows. Your Highness, I speak as the High Priest of the One. We see no magic in the Heartland because there is none left here to draw on—it is all bound up in the Wall. But it exists, and, like water, flows down-hill—from places where there is a lot of it to places where there is little."

"If that were true, how could something like the Wall ever have been created?" Rand shot back, echoing Kelfrick's most telling argument. "Why doesn't all that magic simply flow back into the Heartland?"

"That is precisely what is happening, Your Highness. Gondwain's control of magic was awesome, but a thou-sand years is a very long time." Sartan looked into his wine goblet, then set it aside without drinking. "The Wall is fading, my lords. Already, it has weakened to the point where the Blood Empire can penetrate it with small raiding parties and short-range magical attacks. When it fails completely, those raids and attacks will become a full-scale invasion."

Athelras looked stunned. "The Wall is failing? Will the heavens themselves crash down upon us next?"

"Father, you don't really believe—" Rand began, but the King silenced him with a sharp gesture, his eyes on Sartan.

"The One built the heavens; man built the Wall," the High Priest said. "The heavens may endure forever, but nothing built by man has or ever will."

Athelras sat in the nearest chair, suddenly looking much older than even his white hair and lined face warranted. "Old friend, you drive a dagger through my heart," he said. "The Heartland could not stand against the Blood Empire in Gondwain's time, with all the magic of the land at its disposal. How can it stand now, without magic and an army more used to chasing bandits than fighting battles?"

Rand stepped between Sartan and his father and slammed his goblet down on the table. "Father, he has yet to offer evidence for any of these fantastic claims. The raids and destruction in the south have nothing to do with the 'Blood Empire.' It's the work of bandits, probably from the Desolation. The desert tribes are full of disinherited sons and ambitious warriors seeking their fortune. This band is just better armed and organized than most."

"Show respect," King Athelras growled, a glint of anger in his eyes. "Step away."

Reluctantly, Rand did so, moving to the wall.

Sartan continued as if he hadn't spoken. "Your Majesty, if despair were all I had to offer, I would not have brought you here. All is not as black as it sounds. There is also news of hope . . . news that must not be overheard." He glanced at Rand. "Show me, Prince, how well you have learned the 'myth' of Gondwain. How did he create the wall?"

"This is a waste of . . ." Rand began, but at a look from the King, he subsided. "Oh, very well." He closed his eyes for a moment's thought, then said in a deliberate singsong, "Gondwain consulted with the great wizard Wacundra, and together they fashioned a mighty artifact through which to focus all the magical power of the land. Gondwain took the artifact to the fortress of Bal-zakar, the strongpoint nearest the Blood Empire's approaching forces. For an entire night, the fortress blazed like the sun, and when the true sun rose the next morning, the Wall stood between the Heartland and the Blood Empire, and magic had vanished from the kingdom."

"Succinct, though your delivery needs work," Sartan said. "And what happened to Gondwain?"

"No one knows. He never came out of the fortress, and no one could get near it: its stones were as hot as coals. Out of fear, everyone fled, and today no one even knows where Bal-zakar stood."

"Which brings me to my first piece of news," said Sartan. "The Star Brethren have found Bal-zakar—or rather, one of their servants, a young fighting man named Pellakor, found it for them."

"And I suppose he also found Gondwain's bones," said Rand.

"No. But he found the artifact Gondwain used to build the Wall."

"Then we can rebuild it!" breathed Athelras.

Rand banged his fist on the wall and strode forward again. "I don't believe it! Myths, legends—we should be mounting a force to stop these marauding bandits, not wasting time on mystical moonshine!"

Sartan sighed. "I see a demonstration is going to be necessary."

Rand snatched up his goblet of wine again. "By all

means, demonstrate. What will you do, call Gondwain back from the dead?"

"I think that would be a little extreme," Sartan said drily. "But if I were to show you that magic is real, would that be sufficient?"

"Certainly. But you're going to have to do better than sleight of hand." Rand raised his goblet to drink.

Sartan pointed at the centre of the table and said three harsh words, and at once a tiny flame burst into life, hovering six inches above the polished wood, like a candle without a stick.

Rand's goblet dropped from his hand and shattered on the stone floor as he doubled over, choking on the wine he'd sucked down his windpipe.

The priest glanced at the shards. "I hope that wasn't a family heirloom."

Rand managed to find a half-strangled portion of his voice. "Magic!"

"Precisely." Sartan looked at the little flame dourly. "And if the Wall were whole, I would not be able to do it."

Rand reached for Sartan's untouched wine. "May I?"

"Of course."

The Prince took two large swallows, then carefully set the goblet down and wiped his mouth with the back of his hand, still staring at the flame.

"Will you then be able to use this artifact to rebuild the Wall?" the King asked Sartan.

"Me? No. This—" he gestured at the flame "is the limit

of my magical powers—an old spell I learned from one of the Star Brethren."

"Will they be able to do it?"

The High Priest shook his head. "No. They have rules and legends and superstitions and prophecies in their order that some of my predecessors have gone so far as to label heresy. They believe the artifact has remained hidden because it *chose* to remain hidden, that it has a will of its own. It follows, then, that if it has been found, it must have *chosen* to be found—and therefore, will choose to whom it goes and who may use it. Not one of them will so much as touch it.

"But this servant of theirs, Pellakor, had no such compunction. They told him to leave it in Bal-zakar, if he found it, but he disobeyed. Even now, he is bringing it to us; he contacted one of my priests down south, who sent me the message via carrier bird." Sartan spread his hands. "Pellakor's brother lived in one of those villages the Empire has destroyed."

"Exactly what is this mighty artifact?" Rand asked. "A sword? A helmet? A staff?"

"Did you learn nothing from my instruction?" Sartan asked, frowning. "I'm sure your father could tell you."

For a moment, the King looked very much like a boy caught unprepared in class. "Uh . . . I'm afraid not. Are you sure you ever told *me*, Sartan?"

Sartan thought for a moment. "I'm an old fool," he said. (Rand, though tempted, said nothing.) "The manuscript describing the artifact was only discovered a year or two ago. Your pardon, Your Highness, Your Majesty."

"Then I take it you *can* answer my question?" Rand said.

"Oh, of course. The artifact is a small black carving of a rearing unicorn, supposedly made from a real unicorn's horn. Of course, there are no unicorns in the Heartland now, but by all accounts, there were before the magic went into the Wall."

"How small is 'small'?" Rand asked.

"Very." Sartan held up two fingers, spread a couple of inches apart.

"Can a kingdom really rest on such a tiny thing?" said Athelras.

"If a kingdom can rise or fall on something as intangible as the love of a king for a particular woman, surely it is not hard to imagine it hanging on a thread as slender as this," Sartan said quietly. "And it has only been two hundred years since your ancestor fought a civil war for precisely that reason."

Someone banged on the door. Rand opened it, revealing a scared-looking young man in the yellow tunic of a novice priest. "Your Glory?" he said tentatively to Sartan.

"Come in, Tornel."

Tornel bowed quickly to Rand and Athelras, eyes downcast, then knelt before the High Priest, who gestured him to his feet. "What is it, Tornel?"

The novice held out a message scroll. "A carrier bird just arrived from Nimgar, Your Glory, and as you can see, the message is triple-banded and marked with your seal. I thought it best to disturb you."

"You did well." Sartan took the tiny scroll. "Leave us."

"Your Glory." Tornel bowed again and kept bowing until he'd backed out of the room and Rand had shut the door on him.

As gingerly as though he were handling a poisonous snake, Sartan unrolled the scroll. His face paled as he read it, and he reached out a shaking hand for the goblet Rand had last drunk from and drained it dry.

"What is it?" Athelras said.

"We've lost it," the High Priest said dully. "Someone—Empire agents, of course—killed Pellakor in Nimgar. The unicorn was not found on his body."

"I take it the Empire is unlikely to use it to rebuild the Wall," said Rand.

"It is a thing of power. They could use it against us, to redouble their own magical strength." He rubbed his temples. "Or they could destroy it, and in the process, destroy the Wall itself. To break such a powerful enchantment would take a human sacrifice to the foul gods they worship, but that would hardly deter them." He took a deep breath. "But the Empire may not have it. Pellakor's body had been searched and . . . mutilated, as if whoever caught him could not find what they sought and became enraged. Pellakor may have disposed of it before he died."

"Somewhere in Nimgar?" Athelras said.

"Maybe. Or maybe he gave it to someone else. One of the Star Brethren was seen in Nimgar with a troupe of entertainers the night of Pellakor's death; that same night, he disappeared."

"Without reporting to you?" Rand demanded.

"The Star Brethren are not my priests, Your Highness. They have their own rules. He would report first to his own High Father. I shall, of course, send an inquiry at once, but . . ."

"How long will that take?"

"A day, perhaps longer."

Rand looked at the tiny, flickering flame at the centre of the table. "And in the meantime . . ."

"In the meantime, the Wall grows weaker."

Rand stared at the magical flame a moment longer. Against all reason, it seemed, he had to accept Sartan's tale. One quality of leadership he *did* remember learning at Sartan's feet was the necessity of accepting the world's reality, rather than clinging to one's own dearly held views, should the two come into collision. Very well: magic existed. The Blood Empire existed. The Wall was failing.

The Heartland was in danger.

He turned decisively to his father. "Father, with your permission, I will order the army south and send riders to call up the provincial levies. I would also like to start recruiting here in the city. This festival you have decreed should net us many soldiers."

Athelras nodded. "I'm afraid it must be done." He stood. "Let us put in motion the wheels of war."

Late the next day, a guard on duty at the south gate yawned as he watched a caravan of entertainers in eleven wagons roll through, the last wagon driven by a boy who looked up at him and waved. The guard waved back.

"Third troupe to arrive today," he said to the friend who had just arrived to relieve him at watch. "Shoddiest looking bunch of the lot, though."

"Think *he's* with them?" His friend pointed at a horseman just coming into sight along the broad dirt road that led to the gate through stubbled wheatfields.

The guard squinted. "Him? Red cloak, silver armour . . . no, that's a nobleman, that is. Come to pay his respects to the King."

He yawned again. "Well, I'm off to my wife and supper. Don't fall off the wall."

His friend laughed and gave him a friendly shove toward the stairs, then turned back to watch the red-cloaked horseman ride through the gate.

The rider glanced up at the wall, and the guard saluted him—he had to be someone important, dressed like that—but all he got in return was a cold stare that sent shivers up his spine, and he quickly turned away.

"Glad *I'm* not whatever business has brought him to

Koroth," he muttered, and gazed down the road for the next group of travellers coming to the festival.

Behind him, the hoofbeats of the red horseman's black steed faded away into the noise of the crowded city streets.

CHAPTER 4
THE RED HORSEMAN

Strom's troupe waited outside a guard barracks for half an hour while Strom negotiated with the captain for a licence to perform. Nels didn't mind; he sat on his wagon and watched the crowds of people swarming along the broad, cobblestoned road that led from the main gate to the King's palace.

That palace, set on a hill at the centre of the city, rose like a dream above the humdrum buildings of the lower city. Long banners of scarlet, blue, and gold floated on the breeze above each of its towers. But as for the towers themselves . . . well, Nels had to admit a little disappointment there. "Gleaming" wasn't the word that came to mind. "Grim" seemed more appropriate. And the closest thing to a glittering fountain he'd seen so far had been a scummy horse trough half a block back.

In fact, Koroth looked much like a scaled-up Nimgar, only more crowded and even dirtier. The crowds, however, gave it a festive air Nimgar had certainly lacked. Supposedly, the King had proclaimed this celebration to mark the thirtieth year of his reign, but Nels doubted the people he saw streaming in and out of the inns and taverns that seemed to be the principal type of business on this thoroughfare needed even that much of an excuse to party.

He pulled his waterskin off its hook on the side of the wagon and took a long drink, wiping away the stray bit that dribbled down his chin with an absent-minded sweep of his sleeve, his eyes never leaving the passing crowds.

There were blonde-haired giants from the fishing holds of the eastern seaboard, small, dark men from the grim northern wastes, fat merchants dressed in the distinctive gold-threaded garments of the great guilds of Torin, and lithe, tanned men with the air of proud cats, wearing the flowing robes and headdress of the Desolation tribes.

Many practically dripped gold and gems, and Nels was suddenly uncomfortably aware of his own stained, much-patched shirt and breeches, grimed with all the dust kicked up by the passing of ten other wagons. He tucked the waterskin under his seat and brushed ineffectively at the worst of the dirt.

Soldiers mingled with the civilians, most in the plain dark-green tunics of the royal army, but a few wearing the bright colours of private guards, including the red, blue, and gold of King Athelras himself. Nels thought they all looked magnificent in their glittering mail, and toyed with the idea of leaving Strom's troupe and joining the army, like his father once had, though in his case it hadn't been by choice. "Couldn't be any worse than Strom's troupe," he muttered to himself, then straightened guiltily, though Strom could not possibly have heard him, as the troupe leader came out of the barracks.

"I've got our licence and the name of an inn willing to take us," Strom shouted as he mounted the lead wagon. "We'll set up in the courtyard of the Black Rooster. Straight up the King's Way and right under the walls of the palace. Old Athelras himself could be watching you tonight, boys!"

Nels took up his reins. "If he is, I hope he's in a merciful mood," he murmured.

Because of the crowds, it took them most of an hour to reach the Black Rooster. They passed jugglers, fire-eaters, sword-swallowers, lyre-players, and mimes, all with crowds of encouraging size and enthusiasm surrounding them. Also at work were others less interested in public attention: Nels glimpsed a small boy dodging through the crowd, purse in hand, pursued by a fat, grey-haired gentleman. By the time the others in the crowd realized what had happened, the boy had vanished, leaving the old man shaking his fist in fury at no one in particular.

Pickpockets, cutpurses, and entertainers: they all knew festivals were the ideal place to do business, Nels thought, and resolved to keep the mysterious little unicorn hidden next to his skin where no one would get it . . . at least not without getting him first. He tried to put that unsettling thought out of his mind and concentrate on not running over anyone with his wagon.

Down by the gate, Nels had thought the crowds looked prosperous, but as they neared the foot of Palace Hill, he realized he'd been premature. The rich fabrics and jewellery that had impressed him by the gate would have looked as tawdry as his own clothes alongside some of those he saw on the street here, usually accompanied by liveried guards and servants. Strom must be rubbing his hands together with greedy glee at the prospect of wealthy, generous crowds, Nels thought. *But I'll bet the rest of us won't see an extra penny.*

A sign bearing a lustily crowing black rooster finally appeared ahead of them, attached to the largest inn Nels had ever seen. Above the Black Rooster, tall trees waved amid terraced, grassy lawns, all brown and dead this late in the year, through which the road wound up to the great iron gate of the palace itself. Glittering passersby in satin and silk watched curiously, murmuring to themselves, as the troupe's wagons passed under the sign and swung through a gate in a high stone wall into a courtyard formed by the wall behind them, another at the foot of the Palace Hill, the stables directly opposite them, and the inn itself to their right.

Strom climbed down and went into the inn. Nels jumped down, too, staring at an imperious white stallion tethered outside the stables. The horse glanced at him and then looked away as if he were entirely beneath notice, and Nels wondered if maybe Storm hadn't bitten off more than his troupe could chew.

But Strom came out of the inn, smiling. "The innkeeper welcomes us and bids us all come in for food and refreshment. We'll perform just after sundown, so we have an hour to eat before we have to set up the stage. The inn's grooms will see to our horses."

An hour later, as Nels helped erect the stage and light the torches, the comfortable presence of an excellent meat pie in his stomach had just about convinced him that maybe Strom knew what he was doing after all.

Though the day had been pleasant enough, with nightfall, the temperature plummeted, and Nels had to keep blowing on his fingers for warmth as he assembled his flute in preparation for the performance. From the street drifted the musical cries of Ildor, the troupe's reasonably proficient juggler, out trying to entice people into the courtyard. Already, they had a larger crowd than Nels had ever seen at one of their performances, the members of which kept wandering into the inn in search of warmth and a drink as they waited for the show to begin. No wonder the innkeeper had been happy to host them, Nels thought.

He took his place with the other musicians to the right of the stage, glittering tonight with the gold-threaded curtains used only for special performances. He'd put on his best clothes, which meant a shirt that, though a bit grey, was at least unstained, black breeches, boots of soft grey leather, a grey leather jacket, and his old brown cloak. He wished he could wear his gloves, thin and holed though they were, but the flute required intricate fingering. He sat between the horn player and the fiddler, blowing warm air through his instrument and wishing there were some way he could blow warm air through his whole body.

Strom peered around the back corner of the stage and waved to Kilrik. Nels put his icy flute to his lips, and Kilrik's arm swept up and then down to begin the performance.

Strom had chosen to offer tonight a lewd comedy involving nobles, nobles' wives, nobles' mistresses, and nobles' mistresses' un-noble husbands. Struggling to keep his frozen fingers moving, Nels hardly noticed when the actors' voices trailed away and the crowd fell silent. But he noticed when Kilrik froze in mid-beat and stared over Nels's shoulder toward the courtyard gate. Nels twisted around to follow his gaze and gasped.

The torchlight and swirling crowds he'd seen outside the gate just moments before had vanished. Instead, the gate opened into utter blackness, like a bottomless pit. And behind them—ebony darkness, where Palace Hill should have blazed with light. Even the stars had vanished, though the night had been clear and calm.

The actors stood stunned and silent on the stage, and a frightened muttering ran through the crowd, edging toward panic.

Strom banged open the door of his wagon, where he

had been changing costume. "What the bloody hell—why have you stopped?" he roared.

A voice answered: a voice cold and harsh as cracking ice. "One of you has something I want. I am here to take it."

Through the black maw of the gate rode a horseman, silver-mailed and helmed, cloaked in red, astride a horse so black it might have been carved from the same darkness that gripped the inn.

"Who are you?" Strom's face purpled, and he started forward, huge fists clenched. "How dare you—"

"Be quiet." The horseman thrust a finger at Strom, who clutched his throat and fell to the cobblestones without so much as a whimper, unconscious or dead.

The crackling of the torches seemed loud in the silence that followed, and in their light, the horseman's eyes, all that could be seen of him through the visor of his helmet, shone red as burning coals. He raked the troupe with that smouldering gaze. "Bring it forth," he snarled. "Bring it forth, or I will search you all, one by one, until I find it!"

Nels felt frozen in place. *Someone will come for it*, he had been told, but he couldn't believe Shadow had meant him to give the unicorn to this walking nightmare. Yet if he didn't go forward, the horseman would find it anyway. Nels didn't believe for a moment that he could hide anything from those burning eyes.

"You!" The horseman thrust his finger at Kilrik. "I will start with you. Come forward!"

Kilrik tried to back away, waving his arms as though

giving the ensemble a vigorous cut-off, but the horseman crooked his finger and the musicmaster stumbled toward him across the cobblestones like a jerky marionette.

But he never got there. Like a string snapping, the compulsion vanished, and Kilrik scuttled back to the stage and hid behind it like a whipped dog.

The Horseman rose in his stirrups, glaring around him. "Who dares—"

"I dare!" A second figure appeared in the darkness under the gate, and Nels stared: Shadow.

"A Star Brother." The horseman's voice dripped contempt. "You cannot hope to overmatch me!"

"No," Shadow said quietly. "But I can distract you." His hand lashed out, and something shattered at the feet of the horseman's mount.

Light exploded in the courtyard as though a piece of the sun had fallen there, and the night-black horse reared in terror. A howling wind encircled the inn, and suddenly the darkness beyond the walls was only that of normal night.

"Run, young fool!" Shadow shouted, and without really thinking, Nels leaped up and dashed toward the street, flute still clutched in his hand.

Darkness swirled and coalesced within the courtyard gate ahead of him, but Nels burst through it, feeling a moment's intense cold, then plunged through the crowds on the thoroughfare, earning curses and blows but hardly noticing, listening all the time for the clatter of hooves behind him.

He heard them, but at the same instant, he reached the far side of the street and ducked into a narrow alley along which no horse could possibly ride.

Still, he ran, as the walled houses and pillared businesses gave way to sagging buildings that leaned drunkenly over the narrow lanes he chose, and finally to shacks and boarded-up ruins. When at last he dropped, exhausted, against the brick wall that closed off a short, dead-end street, he gulped air that stank of mildew and sewage, and the festive Koroth of cloth-of-gold and diamond pins might have been a million miles away.

He leaned back against the wall and hugged his knees to his chest, still holding the flute in a death grip. He pressed his face to his legs and shivered, the cold starting to strike through the sweat on his body.

What had he seen? "I don't believe in magic," he whispered, but what other explanation could there be? The inn had been cut off from the world, the horseman had struck Strom down without touching him, Kilrik had been made to walk against his will. Magic was the only word Nels had to describe that kind of power.

But the possibility terrified him. Magic belonged in legends of the distant past, not here and now. If magic were loose once more in the Heartland, then anything could happen—and it could happen to *him*, because magic pursued him.

And what frightened him most of all was the near-certainty that the carved unicorn he had so unwillingly inherited was itself magical . . . so powerfully magical that terrifying creatures like the Red Horseman were now his enemies.

He had to get rid of the unicorn, but how? What could he do with it? Give it to the King? For all he knew, the horseman *served* the King. He knew nothing about King Athelras. He might use the unicorn's power, whatever it was, to enslave them all; might have called this festival in the hope that it would come to him in Koroth.

It made frightening sense to Nels. But it was also possible that the enemies pursuing him were enemies of the King and of the Heartland, and that he *should* give the unicorn to the King. He simply did not know, and how was he to find out?

He dared not throw the thing away, for fear of who might discover it. Until he had the truth, he had to keep it —keep it safe, and keep it secret.

And then suddenly, he tumbled backward into darkness as the wall somehow vanished behind his back, and when he tried to get up, something cold and sharp touched his neck. He froze.

"This isn't a good neighbourhood to nap in," said a soft voice.

CHAPTER 5
DART

Nels had been through too much that day to feel very afraid. "If you're planning to rob me, go ahead; you won't get much. All I've got is this flute," he said to the slim, shadowy figure standing over his head.

The cold point of the dagger left his throat, but he could still see it dimly shining in the starlight. "Keep it. I'm not interested in robbing you; there's better game in the streets. I'm more interested in why you're sitting on my doorstep." The voice was surprisingly high-pitched.

Nels sat up. "You're no older than I am!" he said accusingly.

The knife leaped forward to touch his nose. "I'll still use this if I have to. Answer the question!"

Nels pulled his head back from the blade. "I didn't know it was your doorstep until you pulled the wall out from behind me."

The thief considered, then finally sheathed the knife.

"All right, I believe you. Get out of here. But I promise you, you tell anybody about this place and I'll skin you alive."

Nels didn't move. "Who are you?"

"Nosiness is as dangerous as napping," the thief said coldly. "Go back where you came from."

"I can't."

"Why?"

"Someone's after me."

The thief shot a glance up the alley. "The Guard?"

"Maybe. I'm not sure."

"How close behind?"

"I think I lost him."

"You think? Blazes! You mean he could show up anytime, and you're sitting in front of my hidey-hole? Who the bloody—" The thief stopped for a moment. "All right! You'll have to hide with me, then—for my safety, I don't give a horse apple for your hide. Get inside!"

Nels scrambled up and looked into pitch-blackness. "In there?" he said doubtfully.

"You see anywhere else to go?" The thief shoved him through, then stepped in behind him and did something in the darkness. The wall grated shut with a solid thud, sealing them in.

Nels's host struck a spark and a candle in a niche by the door flickered to life, revealing a large room with no other visible doors. Two heavy black beams held up a wooden ceiling, where a skylight reflected the candlelight from a hundred tiny diamond-shaped panes. Close by the cold fireplace in the far wall stood a wooden cot, a rumpled grey blanket half-covering a thin mattress through whose rotting cloth protruded bits of straw. On the other side of the fireplace stood a three-legged table, its fourth leg propped up with a wooden crate; another crate served as a chair. Against the wall behind the table were piled a few small logs.

A large brass oil lamp hung from the skylight on a chain, and the thief went over and lit it with the candle, then blew the smaller flame out.

As the thief turned around again, Nels saw a boy even younger than he'd thought, slim and brown-haired, with fine, almost pretty features. He wore a surprisingly fine hooded green cloak over leather pants and a brown woollen blouse. He stared coldly at Nels with dark eyes. "I've given you shelter. Now I want to know who you are and why you're running. I don't fancy sharing my quarters with someone I know nothing about. It makes for poor sleeping."

"All right. Uh . . . may I sit down to do it? I ran a long way . . ."

"Be my guest." The thief pointed to the crate at the table and sat cross-legged on the cot.

Nels sat down with a sigh of relief. "My name is Nels. I play the flute for a troupe of actors. And all I know about whoever is after me is that he rides a black horse and wears a red cloak."

His host stared at him. "That's it?"

Nels shrugged. He had no intention of telling an

avowed thief that a lot of dangerous people were after the little carving of a unicorn he wore around his neck. The thief might start wondering how much those people would pay to get it.

"A couple of days ago, while we were in Nimgar, a man was murdered," he volunteered, hoping to satisfy the thief's curiosity without telling him everything. "The people there thought someone in the troupe must have done it. The man I shared my wagon with ran off that same night; maybe whoever is chasing me thinks I know where he is."

"Maybe he thinks you're the murderer."

"I'm not a killer!"

"Flute players can be murderers, too," the thief pointed out. But then he smiled a little, for the first time. "But I believe you."

"Really?" Nels rubbed a hand over his throat, where the thief's dagger had kissed him. "You haven't seemed very trusting so far."

The smile vanished. "Trusting people gets you killed. But I do trust my own instincts. You're harmless."

Harmless? Nels supposed he was, but it almost sounded like an insult. "Great. You trust me. Now, why should I trust you? How do I know you don't plan to kill me in the night and plunder my body?"

"I thought you said you don't have anything worth stealing?"

"I don't."

"Hmmm." The thief got up and took a couple of logs

from the woodpile by the table. "You don't *know* you can trust me any more than I know I can trust you. You'll just have to trust your instincts, too." He put the logs in the fireplace and added kindling from a bag by his bed. Pulling flint and steel from a pouch on his belt, he lit the kindling with practised ease, and as the fire started to grow, put the flint and steel back in his pouch and straightened to face Nels. He spread his hands and grinned. "Do I look like someone who would knife you in the dark?"

The grin made him look very young. *Looking innocent is another way he survives*, Nels told himself, but all the same . . ."No," he admitted. "So I guess it's a deal. You trust me, I'll trust you."

"Deal. You want something to eat?"

The meal at the inn suddenly seemed a very long time ago. "Yes!"

The thief reached up above the fireplace and tugged a loose stone from the wall. From the opening, he took out bread and cheese. "I tried to lift a haunch from a butcher's stall in the marketplace this afternoon, but he spotted me," the thief said cheerfully. "Almost took off my fingers with his cleaver, too." He set the food on the table. "But this should do for now. Help yourself."

Nels didn't have to be told twice. As he ate, the thief reached under his bed and pulled out a jug. "Cheap stuff, but better than nothing," he commented, setting it on the table. "No cups, though—I don't entertain much."

"No problem," Nels said through a full mouth. He

gulped down the bread and cheese, then reached for the jug and downed a few healthy swallows of the bitter wine.

It warmed him marvellously and also made him suddenly sleepy. He yawned, and the thief got up from the cot. "You can have the bed," he said generously. "I've got a couple of extra blankets, and I've slept worse places than the floor."

"Thank you." Nels left the table and sat down on the cot instead, pulling off his boots and stretching out on the hard mattress. He put the flute on the floor by his side, then pulled the blankets over him.

His companion knelt by the bed, pulled two more blankets from somewhere underneath it, spread them by the fire, then blew out the lamp and lay down.

"What's your name?" Nels asked drowsily, the question striking him on the verge of sleep.

"I'm called Dart."

"G'night, Dart," Nels murmured, and slept.

He woke to dim grey twilight. The fire had long since burned out and the cold nipped at his nose.

He raised his head slightly. Dart had vanished. But the weariness of two days of wagon travel and the excitement of the night before put Nels to sleep again before he could even begin to wonder where the thief had gone.

He jerked awake again in a hurry when he felt the cold touch of Dart's knife against his throat for a second time. "Trust me and I'll trust you, he says," Dart growled. "I don't know who's after me, or why, he says. Now tell me why I shouldn't slit your throat!"

Nels lay very still, heart pounding. "I don't know what you're talking about."

"Oh, don't you? Let me fill you in, *friend*." Dart accentuated that last word with a prick of his knife. "I've been out in the streets, asking around. It seems all the Guardsmen in the city are running around like dogs casting for a scent, and they're all looking for *you*."

"Then the horseman *was* the King's man!"

"Don't give me that!" Dart snarled. "You know perfectly well who's after you, and why. You've stolen something they want! You're no innocent caught up in somebody else's crime. And you've made things hot in Koroth for the rest of us. Especially me! They're rounding up every boy on the streets. And that's not all. There are even rumours that this thing you stole is *magic*. It seems the Black Rooster disappeared from the face of the earth last night—and when it came back, you were the first one out of it. Magic, by the One! I spent the night with *magic*?" Dart's knife pressed harder. "You got anything to say?"

"If you'll move your knife so I can talk . . ." Nels whispered.

The pressure lessened just a little. "Make it good."

"The truth, I swear!" Nels prayed he hadn't misread Dart. "I told you some of it. Two days ago, we were in Nimgar . . ."

He told the whole story, this time, but when he finished, the dagger stayed put. "Where is this thing, this unicorn?"

"Around my neck."

"Show me."

Slowly, keeping his eyes on Dart's, Nels reached under his shirt and pulled out the wrapped carving. He took the leather bag off of it and let it drop onto his chest.

Dart poked it with the point of his knife. "Doesn't look like much. I know where I could buy a dozen trinkets with better workmanship." He looked at Nels a moment longer, then suddenly stood and sheathed his dagger. "All right, I believe you. But you can't stay here. Sooner or later, the Guard will find even this place. We have to get out of the city."

Nels sat up cautiously. "We?"

"I told you, the streets are too hot for me now, thanks to you. They'll grab me just because I'm the right age. I'm not sticking around for it."

"So why not just turn me in?"

"I've got no reason to do the Guard any favours. And you haven't done anything except get mixed up in something too big for you. It could just as easily have been someone else. It could have been me."

"You could take the unicorn for yourself."

"Blazes, I don't want it! Magic?" Dart shuddered. "Not bloody likely. And don't expect me to stick around looking after you, either. I don't want to be within a mile of you by sundown. We get out of the city, and we go our separate ways."

Nels grabbed his boots and swiftly pulled them on. "Good enough." He got up and stamped each heel down hard once, then snatched up the flute. "Let's go."

Once outside, Nels expected Dart to lead him toward the main gate, but instead, they headed even deeper in among the winding alleys and ramshackle buildings in which Nels's wild flight had lost him. "The main gate?" Dart said incredulously when Nels asked. "You might as well march up to the palace and turn yourself over. No, we'll use the smugglers' way."

"Which is?"

"Just follow me, and you'll see."

The few people they passed didn't seem to realize the King had decreed a festival. Dressed in rags, they sat hunched in dark doorways or scuttled past without looking up, as if afraid of seeing anything they could be questioned about later.

They passed a dirty inn called—appropriately, Nels thought—the Dead Rat, then crossed a rickety bridge over a ditch through which oozed something foul and green that Nels hesitated to call water. On the other side, Dart doubled back to the stream bank and then, to Nels's disgust, stepped into the chest-deep scum. "Hurry up!" he called back to Nels. "This is dangerous in daylight!"

"Dangerous any time," Nels muttered. He looked at the flute, hesitated, then tucked it securely under his belt and stepped into the ditch. He tried to wade in slowly, but his foot slipped, and he fell in face-first with a tremendous splash. Spluttering and half-sick, he surfaced to see Dart glaring at him.

"Keep it quiet! Now come on!"

Coughing and spitting foul-tasting sludge from his

mouth, Nels followed Dart to where the ditch flowed out of the city through a low hole in the wall, screened on either side by tall green weeds. An iron grill barred the way, but Dart, after glancing furtively around at the blind windows of the sagging buildings surrounding them, reached under the arch and twisted something and the grill slid up into the wall.

"We only have a couple of minutes before it comes back down again," Dart said. "Can you swim?"

Nels looked down at the stinking liquid. "In this?"

"Well, you can always report to the Guard, instead."

Nels sighed. "I can swim."

"Good. The wall's ten feet thick, and the water comes right up underneath it. You won't be able to catch a breath until you reach the other side." He made an "after you" gesture. "So go!"

Nels took two deep breaths, wishing there was some way he could hold his nose and swim at the same time, and plunged beneath the scummy surface.

CHAPTER 6

THE CARAVAN

Jaw clenched, eyes squeezed shut, Nels kicked as hard as he could. He swam until his lungs screamed for air, and then lunged upward, half-expecting to bang his head on the stones of the city wall.

Instead, he burst above the surface and gulped a huge breath—a breath he immediately regretted, considering the smell that came with it.

He felt for the hard lump of the unicorn against his chest, then for the flute at his belt and, assured both were still there, splashed over to the bank and hauled himself out on the dank grass, dripping and shivering and unsurprised to find that the smell of the ditch water followed him, having soaked into his clothes, and, he thought gloomily, probably into his skin, as well. He glanced around and saw that heavy bushes on either side of the ditch hid their exit from prying eyes.

Dart's head broke the water, and he, too, splashed up onto the bank. "I'd think all the Guard would have to do to find any smugglers that used this path would be to walk around the city sniffing the air!" Nels told him, shivering now as the cold began to creep into his bones.

"Smugglers haven't really used it in years," Dart said. He sat down, pulled off his boots, and dumped green slime onto the brown grass. "Now it's just a good way to make a quick, secret exit from the city. Few even know it exists, which is all to the good. My family happens to be among them."

"Your family?" Nels looked up at the towering city wall. "Won't they miss you?"

"No," Dart said shortly. "I take care of myself. I have for years." He pulled his boots on again and stood. "I said I'd help you out of the city, then we'd split up. We're out."

Nels rose, too. "Don't suppose I can blame you." He held out his hand. "Thanks."

Dart looked at it, shrugged, and shook it. Nels turned and looked up at the sun for a moment, judging directions.

"Where will you go?" Dart asked from behind him.

"Home," Nels said. He gazed southwest, across brown, rolling farmland, toward a range of hills, dark with evergreens. Somewhere beyond that . . . Gull Rock. Yet even when he got there, he knew he couldn't stay; he couldn't risk involving his family in whatever he had fallen into, nor could he burden them with an extra mouth to feed. *I shouldn't go there at all,* he thought, but the longing was too strong. He *would* go home one more time. After that . . . his teeth chattered.

"Look, we don't need to split up just yet," Dart said suddenly. "We're both cold. I've got flint and steel in my pouch; we can light a fire right here and no one will see it."

Nels turned his back on the barren fields. "A little warmth would be welcome right now."

"Help me gather wood."

In a few minutes, they sat companionably by a modest but warming blaze, steam rising from their soaked garments—and with it, a double dose of the ditch's smell. Nels coughed. He'd just have to learn to live with it: all his clean clothes were back in the wagon. He held out his hands to the flames. "Tell me more about your family, Dart."

Dart glanced at him through narrowed eyes. "Why?"

"Just being friendly."

"Nosy, more like it." Dart flicked another branch on the fire as though throwing a knife, raising a cloud of sparks. "I don't know who my parents are. There were fifteen of us living in an old house; we all called ourselves family. I don't even know for sure I was born there; I might have been kidnapped.

"But they were still my family. We looked out for each other; everyone chipped in to keep us all fed and alive. I lifted my first purse when I was six, and now I'm the best there is!" He made a quick gripping motion with his hand, then let it fall. "Or I was. Not much game out here."

"How old are you?" Nels asked.

Dart shrugged. "Don't know for sure . . . fifteen, I guess, maybe a year more or less. Old enough. Been on my own for three years. Done all right."

"Why'd you leave your family?"

Dart's head suddenly came up, and he glared at Nels. "You ask too many questions!"

"But—"

"I'm done talking about it. Shouldn't have said anything."

He kicked the unburned end of a stick into the flames.

They sat in uneasy silence a while longer, until Nels finally stood, pulling his still-damp cloak closer around him. "Thanks for the fire," he said.

Dart stayed seated. "How do you plan to eat while you make your way home?"

Nels pulled the flute from his belt and held it up. "I've got this."

Dart looked back at the fire. "One of my fathers had a flute."

Nels looked at him; then, without a word, he sat back down, took the flute apart, poured out a little residual scum, reassembled it, and raised it to his lips.

Instead of the stilted music of Kilrik, he let the songs his mother had taught him flow through his lips and fingers. The melodies brought with them images of home:

the moonlit sea breaking in sudden silver against the rocky shore, seabirds screaming against a scarlet sunset, the white sails of his father's boat catching dawn's golden light, his brothers and sisters playing games and laughing around the fire while sleet lashed the door and wind rattled the shutters. The past two years forgotten, Nels let the music take him home.

But when at last he put down the flute, he still sat by a dying fire under the uncaring walls of the city of Koroth, and he lowered his head to hide his sudden tears from Dart.

The thief stirred. "Thank . . ." He paused and cleared his throat. "Thank you."

"Poor payment for your help," Nels said. "But you're welcome." He stood, returning the flute to his belt. "Farewell, Dart."

But as he turned away, Dart cried, "Wait!" Nels looked back to see the thief kick apart the fire and snatch up his pouch. "Your way is as good as any other," Dart said gruffly, and set off toward the distant hills.

A surprised moment later, Nels followed.

Night came early this time of year; they'd travelled only a few miles when darkness forced them to halt. A grey bank of cloud swallowed the setting sun and moved over the land, making the twilight short-lived and gloomy. "A cheerless night," Nels said.

"Maybe not." Dart pointed ahead to fires flickering among the trees. A horse nickered, answered by another, and a dog barked. "Traders!"

"Do you really think they'll welcome us?" Nels sniffed the air; the ditch-smell still clung. "I wouldn't."

"You have your flute. Maybe they'll feed us for a song."

"Maybe." Nels wasn't convinced, but the promise of warmth and food was too inviting to pass up. He followed Dart toward the camp.

As they drew nearer, he saw a half-dozen large wagons drawn up in a semi-circle. A dozen men passed a wineskin around a huge bonfire, their voices loud and cheerful. But those voices died the moment the boys stepped out from among the trees.

Faces hard to see in the flickering firelight turned toward them, then one man, huge, bald, and with a patch over one eye, rose and strode toward them. Nels took an involuntary step back. "Who are ye and what d'ye want?" the man growled.

His accent marked the man as coming from the city of Torin, on the edge of the Desolation, which meant he was probably the caravan's leader. Nels cast frantically in his mind for the words Strom used when asking innkeepers for permission to set up in their courtyards. "I am the Master Musician Nels, late of the Glorious Troupe of Strom," he said, bowing low. "I seek only to entertain you in exchange for bread and wine and a place by your fire."

The bald man spat, just missing Nels's foot. "Ye don't look much like a master musician to me. More like an apprentice. More like a drowned rat, come to that." His nose wrinkled. "And ye stink, too!" The men around the fires laughed.

"My friend and I had an unfortunate accident," Nels said stiffly. "We would have bathed before coming to your fire, but—"

"And just who is yer friend?" The bald man peered at Dart. "He an entertainer, too?"

"No, just . . . my travelling companion. But I humbly ask hospitality for him, as well, should my playing please you."

"Hmmph." The man looked them over with his one good eye a moment longer, then turned back to the others. "What d'ye say, lads, shall we give him a chance to play for his supper?"

"Aye, why not? Beats hearing old Mallad's worn-out tales!" shouted one, and in a chorus of general agreement, the bald man turned back to Nels.

"Looks like ye're in, lad. Me name's Budal." He held out a massive hand, and Nels took it gingerly, relieved to get his own back still in shape to play the flute. Budal led both of them into the semi-circle of wagons. "The stage is yours," he said, indicating the bare ground.

Nels blew on his cold fingers, then pulled the flute from his belt. He looked at Dart for moral support, but the thief, who'd been strangely quiet since the moment they'd entered the camp, now sat with his head down, picking at a blade of grass.

Nels looked around at his audience, experienced travellers all, drivers and merchants, and for a moment, his mind went blank. What could he play to entertain men like these? He knew only two kinds of music—what Kilrik had taught him and what his mother had taught him. *They might like Kilrik's better*, he thought, preparing to blow, but then paused. *I'm through with Kilrik*, he thought fiercely. *Never again!*

With sudden resolve, he began playing again the tunes he'd learned from his mother, and to his surprise, saw smiles and pleased recognition on the faces of his audience. As he shifted from a ballad to a fast sailor's jig, they even began to clap along.

He played for almost an hour, and when he was done, the men applauded enthusiastically, and Budal came forward, clapped him on the shoulder, and led him to the fire. "Lad, ye may smell bad, but yer playing don't! Sit ye down here, and I'll feed ye a feast!"

Nels sat gratefully on the ground next to Dart, suddenly aware of just how tired he was. "I guess I did all right."

Dart just nodded, and Nels looked at him with sudden concern. "What's the matter?" To his astonishment, Dart suddenly leaped up and dashed away into the darkness.

"Probably sick," Budal said cheerfully, returning with a heaped plate. "I thought when I first saw yer friend he's the sickly type."

"Must be that ditchwater," Nels muttered, and dug into supper.

Dart returned in a few minutes. "Sorry," he whispered. Nels shrugged, but watched him closely for a few minutes. If Dart had been sick, it didn't show in the way he dug into his plate of food.

Budal joined them again. "So what brings ye and yer friend out here in the middle of the night?"

Nels responded with a carefully edited version of recent events. "I decided I'd made a bad deal joining up with Strom and decided to head home," he finished. "Strom wasn't too happy about it, either, which is why I'm staying off the road. I wouldn't want him to catch up with me. You won't tell anybody you saw me, will you?"

"Ye needn't worry, lad, we're coming from Koroth, not going. We're headed to Nimgar. Yer not far off the road, ye know, just a half a mile or so. We'll be getting on it tomorrow. Ye're welcome to stay with us . . ."

"No!" Realizing his protest was a little loud, Nels quickly added, "I mean, well, we want to start heading west before we get much farther south."

"Well, as it happens, the road goes southwest for a day's travel before it swings straight south. And ye needn't worry about Strom. He won't be coming back this way, from what ye say, and if he does, he won't get ye from my caravan!"

Nels didn't like the idea, but he didn't want to arouse Budal's suspicions again, either. "Well, just for a day, perhaps . . ."

"Done. And if ye'll play for us again now, I'll load ye both with a couple of packs with enough food and blankets and drink to see ye clear across the Heartland and back again—twice!"

"Done!" Now that *was* worth the risk of a day's travel on the road, Nels thought. Feeling pleased with himself, he resumed his place by the wagons and launched into the remainder of his repertoire, while the men clapped and the fire flickered on the tree trunks.

The clouds passed with the night; the next day dawned bright and clear. The caravan started out at first light and made good time through the cold morning air, the horse's breath drifting back over the wagons like clouds of blue smoke.

Dart and Nels trudged alongside with new packs loaded with extra cloaks, blankets, food, wine and water. Dart never explained why he had run off from the camp the night before, and Nels, remembering how touchy the thief was about personal questions, didn't bring up the incident. Instead, they discussed the best way to get to the coast and Nels's home, a somewhat fruitless topic since neither of them knew the geography of the Heartland well enough. Strom's troupe had followed the only road that ran through the village, which took them far up the coast before they were able to turn inland. All Nels knew about the terrain lying in a straight line from Koroth to the village was that it was rugged and sparsely inhabited.

"But it'll be easy enough to find the village once we find the coast," Nels said. "We just head south."

"Then why don't we just strike straight west?"

"A little bit south of west would be better, although straight southwest might be too much. We can hardly hit the coast too far south, because the village lies in sight of the Wall." Nels glanced up at the sun, then down at his shadow, to fix his bearings . . . and then forgot what he was trying to do, as his shadow began to dim.

The caravan suddenly stopped in chaos, horses rearing and screaming in terror, and Nels knew exactly how they felt.

Though rising into a cloudless blue sky, the sun was going out.

CHAPTER 7
THE POWER OF THE UNICORN

Nels stared at the sky, darkening as though the firmament were blue milk being slowly mixed with ink—and remembered the last time the world around him had been swallowed by darkness. "The Red Horseman!"

Dart stared at him. "What?"

"The King's man who was after me! Run!" He dashed toward the trees, but darkness rose like a wall of mist before him, thicker than when he had broken through it at the Black Rooster, and when he touched it, a hurricane-blast of icy air hurled him back. Sitting on the ground, stunned, he looked up to see the Red Horseman ride through the wall like a creature from a nightmare.

Behind him, horses screamed, rearing in their traces, and their drivers shouted, voices high and frightened, but the sound seemed somehow remote, disconnected. The only thing real in his universe was the rider towering above him.

The Red Horseman dismounted and stretched out one gauntleted hand, fingers crooked. Through the visor of his helmet eyes—or something—glinted red. "Give me the Unicorn," he growled in a voice like distant thunder. "It is mine."

Nels's body felt as heavy and immovable as stone, but as the Red Horseman leaned toward him, from behind him, Dart cried hoarsely, "Go to hell!" and leapfrogged over Nels's head. Straddling Nels, he lunged with his dagger at those reaching fingers.

The Red Horseman stepped back, regarded the thief for a moment, then clenched his fist and twisted it sharply. Dart flew to one side as though clubbed, crashing to the ground and rolling over and over until he finally stopped, crumpled and still, against a tree stump. The dagger, flung free, stuck quivering into the ground by Nels's boot.

But Nels, free for an instant from the paralysis that had gripped him, reached not for the dagger but for the only weapon he instinctively knew had the power to stop the Red Horseman, if only he could tap it. As the Horseman reached for him again, he snatched the unicorn from inside his shirt, pulled it free of its leather wrapping, and gripped it tight.

Pain exploded in his hand as though he had clutched a live coal. He screamed and would have dropped the unicorn, but his hand wouldn't relax: instead, it squeezed harder.

Light suddenly burst through his closed fingers, outlining every bone, streaming through every tiny opening in distinct rays. The Red Horseman froze—and then Nels's fingers jerked open of their own accord, and the full brilliance of the unicorn blazed in the glade like a second sun.

The Red Horseman staggered back, screaming, the hand that had been inches from Nels's throat now flung across his eyes. The wall of darkness around the caravan vanished, and the Red Horseman stumbled back to his stamping, frenzied horse, pulled himself astride it, and galloped into the forest as though Death itself were at his heels.

Nels stared at the unicorn through slitted, tear-blurred eyes. Already the light was fading, and the pain along with it, slowly at first, then faster and faster. In a moment, both had vanished. The unicorn lay inert and harmless in his palm.

Nels let it drop onto its chain and turned his unmarked hand over and over. Had he imagined that searing heat?

He suddenly remembered Dart and scrambled to his feet.

The thief groaned as Nels rolled him over. "Blazes, that hurt," Dart muttered. He raised a shaky hand to his head and blinked at Nels. "What happened?"

"You didn't see . . .?"

"See what?"

Nels dangled the unicorn on its chain. "This . . . drove him away."

Dart frowned. "Are you sure you weren't hit on the head?"

"I'm telling the truth." Nels unslung the waterskin Budal had provided as part of his supplies and offered it to Dart, who gulped from it gratefully. "If you hadn't tried to be a hero, you'd have seen it."

Dart lowered the skin and wiped his mouth with his sleeve. "Don't remind me."

"Well, thank you, anyway." A sudden commotion of creaks and rattling behind him made him turn around to see the caravan driving off as fast as it could, not even Budal looking back to see how they fared. "I don't suppose I can blame them," Nels said sadly.

"I should follow them," Dart said, shuddering. "Magic!" He tried to get to his feet, and with Nels's help succeeded, though he swayed a little.

"Do you think he's given up?" Nels looked into the woods in the direction the Red Horseman had taken.

Dart snorted. "A King's man? They never give up." He glanced at the unicorn. "But if that thing really drove him off . . ."

"It did."

"Then just maybe you've got something that'll save your neck . . . and mine, too."

Nels tucked the unicorn back under his shirt. He left the unicorn's little leather pouch on the grass where it had fallen; if he needed to use the unicorn to protect them from the Red Horseman again, he didn't want to have to waste time unwrapping it. "You're still coming with me, even after that?"

"I drew a knife on him, remember? At least you have some protection. I don't." He shook his head. "Mad. I've gone mad."

"Well, I'm glad to have you with me, even if you have." Distant hoofbeats sounded up the road, and with a silent glance at each other, they plunged into the woods.

It troubled Nels more than a little that the direction they had to travel was that in which the Red Horseman had fled, but he comforted himself with the thought that the rider, whoever he might be, surely wouldn't try to attack them again the same day he'd been driven off.

Of course, tomorrow was another matter.

They camped that night in a sheltered hollow that would hide their fire from any unfriendly eyes lurking in the dark. Nels sat by the flames, looking at the unicorn in his palm, wondering what secrets it held. It lay as dark and inert as though it had never blazed with light.

"Get rid of it," Dart said suddenly.

Nels looked up. "What?"

"You heard me. Dump it in the fire, or throw it in a river."

"Why?"

"It's obvious, isn't it? That red slug is following the unicorn; he's not following you. How could he? He didn't swim through the smuggler's gate with us. He didn't trail us through the woods. He must have some way of knowing where that thing is."

"How?"

Dart viciously threw a stick into the fire, and sparks fountained up. "Blazes! How do you think? Magic, you idiot. Bloody magic."

Magic. Nels looked down at the little carving. It looked harmless, but of course it wasn't. He knew it had power; hadn't it driven off the Red Horseman? But magic that saved his life didn't seem as terrifying as magic in the abstract, or magic used against him. The return of magic to the Heartland frightened him because magic meant danger and uncertainty—how could you be sure of anything if magic were possible?—but if those pursuing him had magic on their side, he wanted magic on his.

Dart suddenly held out his hand. "May I see it?"

"Uh . . ." Unaccountably, Nels hesitated. Then, angrily reminding himself that Dart had risked his life to save him from the Horseman, he pulled the chain over his head and held out the figurine.

Dart reached for it, but without meaning to, Nels drew it back. "Quit playing games!" Dart snapped.

"Sorry." Nels held it out again, but the same thing happened.

"What the blazes . . ."

"I'm not doing it!"

"Then who is?"

"Look, hold out your hand, and I'll drop the unicorn into it."

Distrustfully, Dart held out his hand, palm up. Nels dangled the stone over it, but no matter how hard he tried, he couldn't force his fingers to release the chain.

"Bloody hell—" Dart lunged for the carving, and though Nels snatched it back, the thief's finger touched it with a glancing blow.

The unicorn flared red, and Dart convulsed, silently, his eyes wide and staring, his face contorted, his body arcing back so sharply his head banged against the ground. Nels scrambled to his feet, horrified; then the terrible spasm passed, and Dart gulped air. The thief lay still, panting, then slowly sat up, his face glistening with sweat in the firelight. Their eyes met. "Maybe I won't hold it just now . . ." Dart said weakly.

Nels could only nod. He stared at the unicorn, hating it now, willing himself to throw it into the darkness, but instead, he carefully put the chain around his neck and dropped the carving back down inside his shirt, where it rested comfortably against his breastbone, feeling warm.

He wondered what would have happened if Dart had managed to actually take hold of the amulet, and shuddered.

It wouldn't let him throw it away. It wouldn't let him give it away. Somehow, when he had invoked its power against the Red Horseman, he had bound it to him—or bound himself to it.

Feeling cold, he wrapped himself in one of the thick blankets Budal had provided, curled up beside the dying fire, and lay staring into it, trying not to think, until sleep claimed him.

He woke to a gentle prodding and a hint of light in the east. The fire had died to a red bed of embers, and thick frost stiffened his blanket.

Dart knelt beside him. "I think I heard something in the trees," he whispered.

"The Horseman?" Nels sat up and stared around into the darkness.

"Maybe."

"Who I am is not important," said a harsh voice behind them, "but who you are and what you are doing on my land is going to be very important—to your well-being!"

As Nels scrambled to his feet, he heard the unmistakable sound of a sword being drawn from its sheath.

CHAPTER 8
THE SEARCH BEGINS

Prince Rand, his royal colours put behind him for unadorned tanned leather and grey woollen cloak, galloped southwest from Koroth. The rutted road flew by under his horse's hooves, but Rand felt like he was standing still; he'd been pushing his steed as hard as he dared all morning, and still there was no sign of the caravan he pursued.

And always on his mind was the doom hanging over the Heartland, the doom that only the Dark Unicorn could forestall.

They had already come near to losing it to the Empire once, at the Black Rooster—under the very walls of the Palace!—but the attempt had been aborted by one of the Star Brethren, a man named Shadow, the one who had been in Nimgar with Strom's troupe.

Shadow had broken the rules of his order by coming to the King with his story instead of reporting first to his own High Father. Rand had listened in awe to the tale of the wall of darkness raised around the Black Rooster, proof of the power the Red Horseman, servant of the Blood Emperor, could summon in his search for the Dark Unicorn. But Shadow had arrived before the Horseman could actually lay his hands on the boy.

"I hoped only to distract him, using a minor spell of light still remembered by the Order, one I had tested earlier as a way to gauge how much magic has leaked from the Wall," Shadow told them. "But the spell—exploded. It must have drawn power from the presence of the Dark Unicorn. It actually dispelled the Horseman's black enchantment for a moment. I yelled to the boy to run. Before the darkness returned, he broke through the gate and dashed across the street."

"What did the Horseman do?" Rand asked.

"I think he would have killed me if he'd had the time, but instead, he galloped out of the courtyard and disappeared into the streets. Just about everybody in the courtyard immediately headed inside for a drink—I'm sure the innkeeper never had a better night of business—and I came here. This matter was too urgent to leave to the glacial workings of the bureaucratic brethren of my order. My lords, you must begin searching the city for this boy. The longer he holds the Dark Unicorn, the greater the danger!"

"For whom?" the King asked.

"For all of us! He received it from a dying hand; a very bad omen indeed. It may have picked up a resonance of death, and that resonance could begin to taint all the magic being channelled through it into the Heartland. If that is so, the evil uses of magic will be far stronger and much harder to battle if the Wall collapses and the Blood Empire invades.

"But even worse, the lad doesn't know what he has, or how powerful it is. If he should somehow use it, somehow tap into its power, it could become linked with him so strongly that only he would be *able* to use it. Our histories agree that once Gondwain tested the Dark Unicorn's power to focus magic in a small way, prior to building the Wall, no one else could touch it, and an agent of the Blood Empire who tried to steal it died horribly."

"Surely that would make it safe from the Empire, then," the King said. "If they could not use it . . ."

"They could still sway Nels to their side," Shadow said grimly. "Or force him to help them. He's only a boy."

"Then what about us?" said Rand. "If he's used the Unicorn, does that mean all hope of rebuilding the Wall is gone?"

"No. But it would mean he would have to do it, which means we, like the Empire, would have to sway the boy to our side."

"Or force him?" said the King grimly.

Silence for a moment, then Shadow said, "Or force him, Your Majesty. If we must. For our need is more grave than the Empire's. We must have the Dark Unicorn and rebuild the Wall, whereas they can still defeat us without its power, much as they'd like to have it."

"What if he is killed?" Rand said bluntly.

Shadow looked down. "Then I will not forgive myself for blindly following the rules of my order and refusing to answer the boy's questions in Nimgar."

"Would you please answer mine?" Rand said impatiently. "Does his death help or hinder our cause?"

Shadow's head snapped up, and he glared at the Prince. "If Nels dies, and he is linked with the Unicorn, the Wall will vanish instantly and all its magic will be loosed into the Heartland—and again, the Empire wins."

"So if they can't convince him to help them . . ."

"They'll kill him. Satisfied?"

The Prince ignored the Star Brother's sharp tone. "I'll organize a search at once. With your permission, Father . . .?"

Directed by Rand, the Guard had searched Koroth from the Palace throne room to the cellar of the Dead Rat. They'd found nothing. The boy had vanished, and so had the Horseman who pursued him.

Shadow had retreated to his quarters and emerged hours later, wan and haggard, to report that he had finally detected the Unicorn's aura, out of the city and heading southwest. Over the objections of the Guard Captain, Rand had packed up and taken to the main road himself, sending other scouts along less-used paths and woodland trails through the surrounding countryside.

He'd found nothing in yesterday's remaining hours of daylight—but early today, he'd overtaken a lone wagon at the side of the road, its axle broken. Two men dropped their tools and drew their swords as he approached.

Rand spread his hands. "Friends, I am no highwayman."

"Can't be too careful, wagon on its own like this," the larger and older of the two said, looking him over carefully and keeping his blade raised. "If you're not here to rob us, then what do you want?"

"I'm searching for someone—a boy, fifteen or sixteen, travelling this road. His name is Nels. He's a head shorter than me, slim, rather shaggy black hair, brown eyes." So Shadow had described him. "Have you seen him?"

"Does he play the flute?" the younger man asked suddenly, earning a scowl from his companion.

"Yes!" Rand sat up straighter in his saddle. "Where did you see him?"

The older man cut off his companion's quick reply. "What's it worth to you?"

"A silver apiece."

The man rubbed his chin, considering, then nodded. "Aye, we saw him. He played for the caravan last night; he came stumbling in out of the woods with a younger boy. They were both filthy and stank, too, like they'd fallen in a sewer, but that Nels played the flute like magic."

"Where's the caravan headed?"

"Nimgar."

Rand reached into his purse and tossed over two silver coins. "Thanks." He reined his horse around and galloped away.

He'd expected to catch up with the caravan quickly, but it had been almost three hours, and still . . .

Then, suddenly, he topped a ridge and there it was, wagons parked in a meadow beside the road, horses watering in the stream that meandered along the valley floor.

Rand galloped down the hill and reined to a stop at the bottom in a cloud of dust, scanning the surprised faces that turned toward him, but seeing no one who matched Nels's description.

A balding, bearded man with an eye-patch came toward him. "And what may ye be looking for?" he demanded.

"A runaway boy," Rand said quickly. "I understand he played the flute for you last night."

An uneasy murmur ran through the drivers, and the leader's eyes narrowed. "Well, if ye ask me, ye should let him keep running. We had more'n enough of him and his young friend this morning."

A shiver of unease ran up Rand's spine. "What happened?"

"Just up the road it was, couple of hours since. The sky blacked up like thunder was a-coming, but it weren't no storm-cloud that did it. Next thing we knowed, we was standing there in darkness black as night. The horses were going crazy, and some of us were, too. And then out of the trees comes this big soldier-type, all done up in mail and red tunic and cloak, riding the blackest horse I ever saw. He climbed down and started toward yer runaway. I thought he was going to kill him, I did, but that young friend of his—Dart, that was his name—jumped in front of the horseman first and drew his dagger. Next thing I knew, Dart was rolling across the ground like a weed in the wind. Then the horseman reached out for young Nels again, and . . ." He paused for a moment, frowning, the effort of thinking squeezing his good eye almost shut.

"And?" Rand prompted, his heart sinking.

"Well, I don't rightly know. Nels grabbed something he had hanging around his neck, and there was this bloody great flash of light, and the horseman took off like a scalded cat—and so did we."

"You left Nels there?"

"I got a business to protect," the caravan leader growled. "I don't need the kind of trouble that kid brought with him."

Rand made an impatient gesture. "Fine. I understand. But Nels was all right when you left him?"

"Him and his friend both. Just a little dazed, like."

"And where did this happen, exactly?"

"'Bout three ridges back, where the trees are cleared a bit farther back from the road than usual—except for one big dead one, right by the track—looks like it's been struck by lightning."

Rand remembered the spot: he'd ridden through it an hour before. "My thanks." He wheeled his horse around and started back up the valley slope.

"I wouldn't go back there for a fortune in gold!" the

wagon leader shouted after him. "That was magic, that was, and I want no part of it!"

"None of us do," Rand muttered, spurring his tired horse to greater speed. "But we're all going to get a bellyful."

Nels had used the Dark Unicorn; he had tapped its power to drive off the Red Horseman. And that meant it was no longer enough to simply retrieve the artifact. Now Nels himself was the quarry, the pawn that both the Blood Empire and the Heartland sought to capture.

Rand could only hope he reached Nels first. At least the Heartland needed Nels alive.

For the Empire, dead was just about as good.

CHAPTER 9
SHOCKS AND REVELATIONS

The man was only a blacker lump of darkness in the pre-dawn chill until he reached forward and stirred the coals with the tip of his sword, and flames and sparks swirled up, revealing a pox-scarred face, partially hidden by a heavy black beard. Piercing grey eyes glared at them from either side of a bulbous nose. The man lifted his sword from the fire and pointed it at the boys. "I want answers."

"We're just wanderers," Dart said boldly. "We mean you no harm. Let us pass."

"Wanderers?" The man spat into the coals, which hissed angrily. "Runaway apprentices, more likely." He stepped across the fire, becoming once more only a menacing black form, his sword blade gleaming in the slowly growing light. "I wonder just how much your masters would pay to have you back?"

"We have no masters." This time, Nels replied. "I'm a

minstrel. Last night I played for a caravan on the King's Road, and now I aim to travel to the coast and play in the villages there for a time. Neither I nor my friend are any threat to you."

"Oh, I believe that," the man said. He sheathed his sword. "But you may yet be of some value!"

Suddenly, his callused hand shot out and gripped Nels's wrist and Dart's arm. But then there was a meaty thump, the man swore, and Dart scrambled away into the darkness. Nels would have tried a kick of his own if not for the knife blade that suddenly bit at his throat. "If he's really your friend, he'll be back anyway, won't he?" the man growled. He dragged Nels back to the fire and threw two or three more branches onto the embers. As flames licked up, his ravaged face again took shape in the darkness. "Now then, my boy, let's see what you've got." Keeping the knife hovering near Nels's neck, he rummaged in the packs lying by the fire, discarding every-thing he found helter-skelter across the frosty ground until he came on Nels's flute. "Here now, maybe you were telling the truth," he said, waving it in Nels's face.

"I was."

"Doesn't matter." The man held the instrument up and squinted at it cross-eyed. "Pretty thing. Should be worth something." He set it aside, then rummaged some more, but found nothing he wanted. "Pretty poor pickings, boy," he growled, giving one of the packs a kick. "Got anything else on you?"

Nels stood stiffly as the man ran his hands roughly

over his body, but his heart leaped into his throat as the robber stopped with one hand on his chest, right over the lump made by the unicorn. "Ah, got something now, haven't I?" the man crowed. He grabbed the silver chain and pulled it over Nels's head, then held the unicorn up, examining it in the firelight. Nels raised a hand to reach for it, but the knife nicked his throat, and he froze again. "More valuable than it looks, is it?" The man peered at it more closely, twisting the chain so the carving spun, its strange black surface reflecting nothing of the fire. "What is that stuff?" he muttered, and then, to Nels's horror, he flipped it into the air and caught it, his hand closing around it in a fist.

The unicorn blazed with scarlet light, turning his hand the colour of blood. He made a sound like a scream choked off almost before it began, and his whole body went stiff in a spasm so abrupt his knife almost slashed Nels's throat. As Nels stumbled back, the robber toppled like a felled tree. His back arched once, twice, and then he was still.

Birds sang to greet the growing light.

Nels felt too weak to stand, but against his will, he crawled to the body of the robber, who lay stiff on the frozen ground, every muscle still taut in that horrible rictus of pain, dead eyes staring at the greying sky. Nels found himself prying the dead fingers from around the unicorn, and only when it was in his hand again did he gasp and scuttle back to sit huddled in shock a few feet away, holding the unicorn tight against his chest and staring at the corpse as daylight grew around him.

Numb, his mind almost blank, Nels didn't notice the return of Dart until the other boy slowly sat down beside him. "It killed him. It killed him!" Dart whispered.

Nels raised the unicorn to his eyes and slowly opened his fingers, staring at it. The carving was again dark and as lifeless as the man who lay only a few feet away.

What horrible thing had he been cursed with? For it was a curse, it had to be; it had brought him nothing but pain and terror since the dying man had thrust it into his hand and begged him to run.

But what made it even more of curse was that he couldn't be rid of it; it wouldn't let him throw it away, and now, he knew, it would kill anyone who tried to take it from him.

Whatever power it had belonged to him alone, and having seen that power at work, the thought horrified him. He had been given a terrible instrument of death. He had become a killer.

Those first tentative notes of birdsong became a chorus from a thousand avian throats as the sun rose above the horizon, and still the two boys sat there, looking at the dead man. Finally, Dart stood and put his hand on Nels's shoulder. "No blazing good just sitting here," he said gruffly. "Let's go."

Nels didn't move. "You shouldn't stay with me. You should get as far away from me as you can. I'm a murderer."

Dart's hand dropped away. "A what?"

"A murderer!" Nels pointed at the corpse of the robber. "I killed him, as surely as if I slit his throat!"

"No!" Dart knelt in front of Nels and shook him by the shoulders. "No! You didn't kill him; his own greed killed him. If he hadn't tried to rob you, he'd still be alive!"

"You'd be safer on your own," Nels muttered, staring at the ground.

Dart hauled him to his feet. "Blazes, I know that. But what would I do for excitement?"

Despite everything, Nels smiled a little at that.

Dart punched his arm playfully. "So let's be on our way. You're heading home, remember?"

The thought lifted Nels's spirits. Though he knew he wouldn't be able to seek any advice or comfort from his parents without endangering them, perhaps for a few days, at least, he could pretend that everything was as it had been before he made the mistake of running away with Strom. "I remember." But then he looked at the robber's corpse, and his smile faded. "Shouldn't we bury him or something?"

"With what?" Dart kicked the stony ground. "We couldn't dig a foot deep in this soil if we had pickaxes." He shrugged. "Besides, I doubt anyone's grieving over him. Leave him to his own kind—the wolves."

"You're a thief, too."

Dart glared at him. "I was a pickpocket and cutpurse, not a robber. I never threatened anybody!"

"Funny, wasn't that your knife at my throat when we met?"

"Speaking of which, do you know you're bleeding?"

Nels touched his throat. "Just a scratch. It's almost stopped. And you didn't answer my question."

"Are we leaving or aren't we?"

Nels gave up. "We are." He helped Dart pack up their scattered belongings, then resolutely turned his back on the dead robber.

But the unicorn seemed to drag on his heart like a lump of ice-cold lead.

As the sun rose, so did the temperature, as a gentle wind blew spring-like air found in some distant treasure house across the frosty landscape. By mid-afternoon, as they crossed a valley in the range of forested hills that separated the interior of the Heartland from the coast, the day was almost summery—and their clothes began to once more release the scent of the ditch through which they'd escaped Koroth.

Dart paused as they neared the valley floor and pointed south. "Is that smoke?"

Nels shaded his eyes. A quarter of a mile away, a copse of evergreens grew on a rocky outcropping. A grey haze rose above the trees . . . a haze in which he caught a fleeting glimpse of a rainbow.

He let out a whoop. "That's no fire! Come on!"

A few minutes later, they pushed through the trees and emerged on the edge of a rocky pool, its edge facetted with crystals like precious gems. Steam rose from the surface of the water.

"What is it?" Dart asked in bewilderment, staring at the water.

Nels had already pulled off his shirt and was working on his breeches. "Hot springs!" He dropped the last of his clothes on the shore and, wearing only the unicorn, splashed into the pool. "Come on!" he shouted back at Dart. "We can finally smell like civilized people again!"

The deliciously hot water tingled against his skin, stinging and then soothing cuts and scrapes he'd hardly known he'd had. Even the muscles that had been aching from the unaccustomed strains of walking long distances felt rejuvenated. He plunged under the surface, then popped back up again with an exuberant shout, shaking streams of water from his hair. Standing in the chest-deep centre of the pool, he shouted to Dart on the shore, "What are you waiting for?"

"Too blazing hot!" Dart shouted back irritably. "I'm not boiling off my tender rear!"

"You'll get used to it!"

"I'm not coming in! Now hurry up, and let's get going!"

Nels shook his head, then suddenly grinned as a mischievous thought occurred to him. He called, "All right, have it your way. But I'm the one who's going to have to put up with your stink."

"You'll live."

Nels shrugged and walked toward the shore. Dart sat

on a boulder on the bank, feet dangling over the water, not looking at him.

Nels's grin widened. Perfect. He casually walked toward Dart, who didn't look up. "Sure you won't reconsider?" he asked as he came close.

"We're wasting time!" Dart snapped, still not looking at him.

"I don't think so!" Nels suddenly grabbed Dart's foot and hauled him off the rock and into the water with a tremendous splash. "Now you're either going to get clean or drown!" Nels promised and launched himself at Dart, trying to pull off his clothes.

But Dart fought back with a furious rage that startled Nels, shoving him away so hard he lost his footing and fell, sitting down painfully on the crystals just under the water. As Dart stalked up on shore, dripping, and turned furiously to face Nels, he scrambled up again, getting angry in his own turn. "What's the matter with you?" he demanded. "Do you only swim in sewers?"

Dart brushed blonde hair from his eyes. "I don't want to take off my clothes!"

Kriss blinked. "But—why?"

Dart glared. "Because I'm a girl!" And then she spun away.

Nels stared at her back for one astonished moment, and then suddenly hot blood rushed to his cheeks and he backed up so fast he fell again, then scuttled crablike back into the centre of the pool. "I don't believe it!" he shouted

Dart turned again. "Then why are you hiding out there?"

"Uh—" Now that she'd told him, it made sense. The delicacy of her features, the way she moved, her voice, everything should have tipped him off before—he'd just assumed she was a boy because she dressed like one, and he'd never imagined a girl pickpocket who lived on her own in the streets.

He shook his head. *A girl!* He watched as she sat on the boulder, this time taking off her shoes and dangling her feet in the water. "Can I come out now?" he called finally, when she showed no sign of moving.

"What's stopping you?" Dart called back.

"I'm naked!"

She smiled sweetly. "I know."

He could feel himself blushing again and countered it by furiously plunging his head under the water. "I'd still appreciate it if you'd turn around!" he yelled when he'd resurfaced.

She laughed and turned her back. "All right. Come on out. But if you really expect to smell any better, you're going to have to either burn those clothes you've been wearing or wash them."

He waded ashore cautiously. "I know that." The air didn't feel nearly as summery now that he was wet; shivering on the rocky beach, he quickly opened his pack and got out a blanket, wrapping it around his shoulders. "All right, you can turn around."

She did so and watched with some amusement as he washed his clothes, trying to keep the blanket from slipping as he did so. "*You're* still going to smell bad," he pointed out to her finally.

"Not too bad." She suddenly turned and ran fully clothed into the water, and splashed around in it for several minutes while Nels pounded his own clothes with rocks and finally laid them out to dry, and then began lighting a fire.

When Dart finally came splashing out of the water, the fire was burning, and Nels, huddled in his blanket, was cooking some of the porridge Budal had given them. "You should get out of those wet clothes," he observed.

"I know." She picked up a blanket and disappeared into the trees.

She came back a few minutes later, wrapped in her own blanket and carrying her clothes, which she laid on the rocks near the fire, close to his. He served her a portion of the porridge and some bread and cheese, and then they sat quietly as darkness fell, watching the flames. "We'll have to take turns keeping the fire burning tonight or those clothes will never dry," Nels finally said. Dart's blanket had slipped away from one bare shoulder; he quickly looked away.

"Uh-huh."

After more silence, Nels asked, "So why did you do it?"

"Do what?"

"You know what. Why did you pretend to be a boy?"

Dart pulled her blanket tighter and said nothing for

such a long time that Nels thought she wasn't going to answer. But finally she said in a distant voice, "When I was twelve years old, one of my 'mothers' sat me down for a talk. She said that I was old enough to quit lifting purses. She said it was time to earn my living and contribute to the family the same way she did. And then she told me just what that meant."

Dart raised her eyes to Nels, and their gazes locked. "I wouldn't do it," she said. "Ever. I told my 'mother' that. She said I'd do as she said, or I could leave the family and find out just what happened to a girl on her own in the streets.

"I went to my 'fathers.' They told me I either paid my way or got out. So I got out. I left the family . . . but not as a girl. I became a boy as far as everyone but my family was concerned, and at least they gave me that much: they never talked. No one else has ever known . . . until now."

Nels stirred the fire with a stick. "I won't tell anyone," he said softly. "And don't worry—I'll protect you."

"Blazes!" Dart exploded. "You see why I became a boy? 'I'll protect you.'" She mimicked Nels's tone perfectly and savagely. "Blazing, bloody hell! From what I've seen, I'm more likely to protect you!" She pointed a stiff finger at Nels. "You listen to me! Forget I'm a girl. Don't call me a girl, don't treat me however you think a girl should be treated, don't even think of me as a girl. I'm a boy to you and to everyone else in this bloody world, and I take care of myself! I don't need anyone!"

She threw herself onto the ground and rolled over. Nels looked at her stiff back and slowly smiled.

Whatever she said, there was no way he was *ever* going to forget she was a girl.

CHAPTER 10
HOMECOMING

Dreams troubled Nels in the night, endless nightmares of towering waves of darkness crashing over the land while fanged and slavering monsters gibbered around him and prodded him with swords and sticks. And when he jerked awake in the early morning, it was with the dying scream of the robber in his ears.

He found himself clutching the unicorn carving tightly and jerked his hand open, letting the amulet drop onto his chest.

He sat up and looked around. In the clear sky's grey light, he could see Dart lying sound asleep on the other side of the dead fire, only her hair and a hint of forehead visible above the blanket's edge. Despite their intentions, they had both slept. He reached for his clothes and found them a little damp, but dry enough to put on. A heavy, slowly seething mist hung low over the hot pool.

Nels dressed quickly. Dart stirred and opened her eyes as he knelt down to get his canteen from his pack, and he grinned at her, feeling marvellously cheerful now, the terrors of his dreams fading away in the crisp light and air of a beautiful winter's day. "Good morning."

"G'morning," she mumbled.

Nels went down to the pool to fill his canteen; it might be warm and smell slightly of sulphur, but at least it was wet. He returned to the ashes of the fire to find Dart up and dressed and digging in her own pack for something to eat. "Not much left in here but lint," she grumbled as Nels sat down again. "How much further?"

"Two days, maybe three. The supplies will last that long."

"Sure, if you can eat stale bread and mouldy cheese. And what's this?" She pulled out a greasy lump wrapped in cheesecloth.

"Summer sausage," Nels said cheerfully. "Never spoils."

"Looks like it's already spoiled."

"Chin up, my boy—er, girl." Dart glared at him, and he laughed. "Day after tomorrow, my mother will fix you the best supper you ever ate." He stirred the ashes of the fire with a long stick, and finding a few live coals, stuck a piece of bread on the end of the stick and began to toast it.

Dart sat cross-legged, elbows on her knees and chin on her fists, watching him. "You sound like you really love your family," she said.

"I do. Didn't you love yours?"

"Love?" Dart picked up her own stick and poked it into

the coals. "I don't think so. They were just there. They fed me and kept me warm—but when I wouldn't go to . . . work . . . No. That wasn't love. When I left, I didn't see any tears."

Nels inspected the bread. "Not even your own?"

"Especially not my own!" Dart hurled the stick away. "Blazes! What business is it of yours, anyway?" She jumped up, grabbed her own canteen and stalked off toward the water.

Nels looked after her, then shook his head and pulled the toasted bread off the stick, pressed a bit of cheese onto it, and bit into both. They had a long way to walk, and he didn't intend to start on an empty stomach.

Dart came back a few minutes later and, without a word, cut a slice off the summer sausage and bit into it, making a face but taking a second piece just the same. Nels silently offered her a piece of bread, and she took it with a muttered, "Thanks."

Breakfast finished, they shouldered their packs, Dart still silent and morose, and headed southwest once more.

All morning, Nels kept glancing behind, but as the day wore on and there was no sign of pursuit, he finally stopped, instead setting his eyes on the horizon, where his heart already leaped ahead.

Dart hardly spoke all day, and when they camped that night, she ate quickly and rolled herself up in her blanket almost at once, though Nels was sure she was not asleep.

In the darkness, he remembered his dreams of the evening before, and sleep retreated. After lying on his back for several minutes, gazing up at the stars, Nels finally rolled over, reached into his pack, and pulled out his flute. Sitting cross-legged on his blanket, he ran his tongue over his lips, thinking; then he raised the flute and began to play.

He began with light, bouncing music, folk dances and humorous songs, thinking they might lift Dart's spirits, and couldn't do his any harm, either. But he soon forgot about Dart and played only for himself, moving on to the soft ballads and haunting melodies of courtly love his mother had taught him. He felt as if he were playing himself closer to home, filling his mind with good memories that left no room for black thoughts of the unicorn.

Sometime in the course of playing, he closed his eyes; when at last he lowered the flute and opened them again, his eyes met Dart's, bright in the firelight. For a timeless moment, their gazes locked, then Dart turned her back on him again.

Suddenly very tired, Nels put away his flute and wrapped himself in his blanket, falling at once into a deep sleep where his only dreams were pleasant ones of the past.

The next day, Dart's black mood seemed to have lifted. As they walked, she asked Nels questions about his home, and he told her everything he could about the wild coast: about storms that hurled the ocean against the shore with terrifying force, about glorious sunsets of scarlet and orange, about magical, moonlit nights and mornings when the rising sun turned mist and quiet sea to pure gold.

He told her about his family: about fighting with his brothers and sisters and also fighting for them against other youngsters in the village, about the time his oldest brother saved him from drowning when he fell off the boat one blustery spring day, and about the time his little sister spent hours painstakingly sewing a lopsided jacket for him, and how proudly he had worn it until he outgrew it.

That night by the fire, he told her how his mother had taught him to play the flute, and about his tenth birthday, when she had given him the precious silver instrument he still carried. And then he played for her again, and this time, when he finished, Dart did not turn away. "When we come to your village, will . . . will your family welcome me?" she asked in a very low voice. "After all, I'm a thief . . . and a girl! What will they say when they learn you have been travelling across the Heartland with a girl?"

"I've only been travelling for a couple of days with a girl," Nels said, grinning. "The rest of the time I was with a boy, remember?"

"Blazes, I'm serious!" Dart snapped. "They might think . . . well, you know!"

"I'll tell them the truth," Nels said simply.

"And they'll believe you?"

"Of course!"

Dart shook her head. "Trusting lot. You wouldn't last a day in Koroth."

Nels played a final bird-like trill on the flute, then packed it away. "Trust goes with being a family," he said, and lay down to sleep.

The mild weather vanished that night as a howling northwest wind swept across the Heartland, bringing a cheerless morning of bone-chilling cold under a rack of tattered, streaming clouds.

"We should reach the coast today!" Nels shouted above the wind as they shouldered their packs and started off, blankets wrapped over their cloaks for extra warmth.

"But we could still be miles from your village!" Dart shouted back.

"I don't think so! Look!" Nels pointed south. "See it?"

"That bank of dark cloud?"

"That's no cloud! It's the Wall! I think we're about five miles farther north of it than my village is. If we angle just a little bit south of west, we should strike the coast within just a mile or two of home!"

"I hope you're right!" Dart yelled. "Blazes, that wind hurts!"

"You've been spoiled by having all those buildings around you all your life!" Nels shouted back and gave her a grin. "Welcome to the real world!"

They moved on through the scrubby forest, the wind whipping the blankets around their legs and making it hard to walk. The overcast deepened as the day wore on, and occasional flurries of sleet-like snow swept over them, stinging their faces, driving into every crack of clothing.

Just after noon, Nels stopped Dart with a hand on her shoulder. "Listen!"

"All I can hear is the blasted wind!"

"Then your ears are plugged. Can't you hear that thunder?"

"Thunder?" Dart searched the skies. "A storm?"

"Not up there! Come on!"

Nels hurried forward up a slight rise, hearing her curse, then come scrambling after him. They reached the top together.

On the other side, the ground fell away sharply to the sea, where towering waves crashed against the rock-strewn shore with a force that shook the earth beneath them. "I recognize this cove!" Nels shouted, a wide, wild happiness swelling in his heart. He pointed south. "Two miles, no more, and we'll be home! Come on!"

He hurried off twice as fast as before.

"It's about bloody time," Dart yelled after him. "I'm freezing!"

When she'd caught up with him again, he pointed to a distant out-thrust cliff. "Just the other side of that point," Nels said eagerly. "And everyone will be home, too—no fishing on a day like this! I can't wait to see the look on my mother's face . . ."

"Neither can I," Dart muttered.

"You've got nothing to worry about, I tell you!" Nels grinned at her. "You'll love my family, and they'll love you."

"Right now I'd love anyone with a warm house."

Nels laughed. "Only a few more minutes."

But as they neared the point, he scanned the sky ahead, frowning. "That's odd," he said. "No smoke . . ."

"The wind's too strong," Dart pointed out. "You couldn't expect to see it."

"I suppose so." But for no reason, Nels suddenly felt even colder than the wind, except for where the unicorn touched his skin, pulsing with strange warmth. He reached inside his shirt and pulled out the carving. It glowed faintly orange.

He stopped, staring at it. "Why is it doing that?" Dart demanded.

Nels looked up wildly. Somehow, he knew the unicorn wasn't *using* magic; it was only *reacting* to mage—strong magic, nearby. And nearby meant . . ."The village!" he said in a choked voice, and dashed forward, scrambling up the last few feet of the steep rise on his hands and knees. But when the cove beyond came in sight, he froze, staring in horror, as the unicorn blazed against his chest.

The village was gone. Grey ash drifted like snow and whirled in tiny tornadoes across the blackened ground of the horseshoe-shaped cove. Of the tidy wharf, only a few blackened poles remained above the waves. Charred boat hulls lay smashed twenty feet above the line of high tide. And the houses—here or there, a few chimney bricks still stood one on top of the other, or half a wall, but that was all.

"No," Nels moaned, then screamed, "*No!*"

He ran down the slope, slipping and sliding through

the scorched grass. "Nels, come back!" Dart shouted behind him, but he hardly heard her. He could see the blasted ruins of his family's home, and he had to know . . . was his family still there? His mind rebelled at the thought, but still he ran, through ash that rose in choking clouds, past the splintered charcoal stump of the tree in whose shade he used to sit and watch for his father's returning boat, past ruined houses that had once held childhood friends and enemies. The wind howled through the shattered chimneys like an anguished ghost.

He kicked something as he ran and ground to a terrified halt as a broken, blackened skull rolled across the cobblestones of what had once been the village square, coming to rest against the low stone wall surrounding the well. He stared around in horror, and saw other skulls and pieces of skeletons, and with terror clutching his heart in an icy fist, he ran down the short lane that ended where his home had once stood. He plunged in among the tumbled stones and charred wood that were all that remained, searching the rubble frantically for any sign of his family's fate, dreading every instant what he might find.

When Dart reached him some time later, he sat with his back to the one bit of wall still standing, black with soot, tears cold as icicles coursing slowly down his cheeks. "I can't find them," he told Dart in a broken voice.

"Then they may still be alive."

"But I don't know! How can I live without knowing?" He looked up at her. "Dart, where do I go from here? This house was my refuge. Once I got back here, everything was going to be all right. Instead . . ." His voice trailed off. "*Who did this?*" he suddenly screamed.

His voice echoed off the cliffs, but he received no other answer.

"You know what scares me the most?" he went on hoarsely a moment later. "Magic did this. The unicorn knows it." He touched the carving, still glowing with its strange inner light. "What if whoever struck here was hoping to find me? What if this is all my fault?"

"Blazes, don't be stupid!" Dart gestured around her. "Anyone with this kind of power would have made sure you were here if you were the one they were after." She looked southward, where the Wall rose black and forbidding in the westering rays of the sun. "Even in Koroth, I heard rumours —rumours that something had been attacking isolated villages near the Wall. Bandits, some said. But others . . . they said the Blood Empire had found a way through the Wall. It scared the crap out of everyone." She kicked savagely at a bit of charred timber. "With good reason, it seems."

"The Blood Empire to the south and the King's Red Horseman on our trail." Nels lay his head back against the wall and closed his eyes. "Maybe I should just stay here and wait to see which one finds me first."

"And maybe you should quit feeling sorry for yourself and start looking for your family!" Dart snapped.

Nels's head snapped forward, and he glared at her. "What do you know about it?"

"Blazes, Nels, I know everything about it! At least you had a family, and maybe still do—I didn't, not really! You've been telling me for three days how much you love them and how you all stick together and look out for each other—well, blazing hell, get up and prove it! You can't find their bones? Fine! Then assume they're still alive. Suppose they heard about other villages being attacked and decided to run before it could happen here. Where would they go?"

Nels swallowed, cut by her tone but knowing she spoke the painful truth. Whatever fate had in store for him, right now, his family came first. "North," he said, getting to his feet. "Not south, obviously, and there's nothing inland for a hundred miles. They'd go north, to Petra. It's about twenty miles up the coast."

"Then I suggest we follow them."

Nels nodded, not trusting his voice anymore. He reached out awkwardly, taking her hand. "Thank you."

She squeezed his fingers in return, meeting his gaze for a moment, then suddenly let go and turned away. "Come on. We've wasted enough time in this ash heap."

The wind felt twice as cold as before when they reached the top of the headland and again felt its full force. In the gathering darkness, Nels paused and looked back at the ruins below for a long moment; then he took a shuddering breath, started to turn northward again—and stopped, staring east.

"What is it?" Dart asked.

"A light," Nels said in astonishment. "It looks like lamplight—but there's no house up there."

Dart peered in that direction. "There is now. I can just make it out."

"It must have been built since I left," Nels said. "Whoever lives there may know something!"

"How come a single house survived?" Dart asked suspiciously.

"I don't know. But we won't find out standing here." With new hope in his heart, Nels led the way inland.

CHAPTER II

ON THE TRAIL OF THE UNICORN

Rand was in a foul mood by the time he reached the clearing where the caravan had been attacked: his horse had caught its leg in a twisted root and come up lame. Not a serious injury, but Rand knew the animal wouldn't be able to carry his weight again until the next morning, at least—and all the time, Nels and the Dark Unicorn drew farther and farther away.

Seeing a black-clad man sitting against a tree as he led his limping horse into the clearing did nothing to improve his mood. "Shadow! What are you doing here?"

Shadow spread his hands. "I've come to join your quest, of course. You should never have left without me."

"I am perfectly capable of tracking two boys through the woods," Rand snapped. "Why do I need you?"

"*Two* boys?" Shadow raised an eyebrow. "It's not the boys we're after; it's the Dark Unicorn. And only I can track it." He got to his feet. "What's more, I know its lore, what little is still remembered. Such knowledge could prove vital."

The Prince couldn't argue with that, so he changed the subject. "How did you know to wait for me here?"

"The Dark Unicorn was here; I can sense it. I knew you would have to start your quest from this point."

Magic. It still made Rand uneasy, but it pervaded the whole bizarre business. "Nels drove off the Red Horseman using the Unicorn's power," he told Shadow bluntly. "If what you told us is true . . ."

"It is." Shadow stared into the forest. "If Nels used the Unicorn like that, it's attuned to him. No one else can use it now."

"And if he's killed . . ."

"It is useless to both us and the Empire—but the Wall will still fall." Shadow got to his feet. "We waste time."

"We can't go anywhere until tomorrow." The Prince pointed to his horse.

"Tomorrow!"

"The time lost will be more than made up by having a mount later. Now answer my question." Then he raised his hand. "No, wait. Better yet, tell me the full history of this 'Dark Unicorn.' So far, I've only heard it in bits and pieces from Sartan and you."

Shadow seemed about to protest, but must have read something in the Prince's face that made him think better of it. Instead, he said, "Very well, my lord." He took a deep breath. "Wacundra, the greatest wizard of the ancient age, created the Dark Unicorn. Rather than use it himself, he gave it to Gondwain, because of Gondwain's great strength of will: the will of the user is the most important aspect of magic. The Unicorn is carved from that most magical of substances, the horn of a black unicorn, and—"

"I've heard all this," the Prince interrupted.

"You asked me a question, I'm answering it," Shadow snapped. "I'm telling you what I know. I cannot judge beforehand what you have already heard. Now, do you want me to continue or not?"

The Prince grimaced, but nodded.

"Thank you. The Kingdoms of the North, which included the many countries that now make up the Heartland, were warring among themselves as usual when, from the south, came a mighty invading army. Unable to put aside their petty differences, many kingdoms had already fallen when Wacundra consulted with Gondwain, then war-leader of the High King—a man who, though all the northern kings swore allegiance to him, held little more than figurative power. The Blood Empire's success depended on its magical might as much as the force of arms. The Empire could draw on all the power of all the wizards in its far-flung outposts and channel that power through one man, a wizard named Zildapest. The northern wizards, limited to their individual powers, could not hope to stand against him. He could control the weather, summon demons to fight for him, even call down lightning on the armies arrayed against the Empire.

"Wacundra felt he could challenge Zildapest if the

northern wizards' powers could be likewise focused in him, but like their respective kings, the other wizards did not trust each other or Wacundra enough to give up their own power willingly.

"So, Wacundra fashioned the Dark Unicorn and, drawing on ancient, dangerous spells, endowed it with the power to draw all the magic in the northland to itself, draining wizards and wands, rings and staves--everything.

"It killed him, of course, for he was very old, and only magic kept him alive. When the magic died, so did he. But Gondwain lived, and the Dark Unicorn was his. He tested it once, using a small fraction of its power in a minor skirmish, and destroyed the Empire forces with ease. The Empire sent an agent to steal it, but although he actually got his hands on the artifact, he died horribly when he touched it. It had become attuned to Gondwain, so only he could use it.

"Gondwain felt that merely using the Unicorn in battle, one-on-one against Zildapest, was too dangerous, for if he should somehow be killed, the north would be defenceless. He chose instead to use the Unicorn's power to create the Wall, an impenetrable barrier stretching five hundred miles from coast to coast. He poured his will and his soul into the effort, and it claimed his life. In the wake of that sacrifice, the northern kingdoms united under the High King and the Heartland was born.

"But strong though Gondwain's will was, the Wall

could not last forever. His life force has faded from the Dark Unicorn enough that the Wall is crumbling, and magic is flowing back into the Heartland. And every time the Unicorn is used, the Wall is weakened further. The power it released in the clearing when Nels drove off the Red Horseman was not drawn from what has seeped back into the land, but that which is still stored in the Wall. And when anyone else uses magic near the Unicorn, that also weakens the Wall, for the Unicorn augments any spells cast in its vicinity with power from the Wall—that's why the minor light spell I used in the courtyard of the Black Rooster had so much force.

"If we do not find Nels soon, and somehow get him to do what must be done, it will be too late; too much magic will be lost, and the Wall will vanish. And then the Empire will overrun us."

"Even if we do find the boy, can he do what we ask?" Rand asked. "He is not Gondwain. And even if he *can* do it, it will not last another thousand years. It will crumble again, and next time there may be no stopping it. Sooner or later, we will have to fight the Blood Empire."

"The Blood Empire cannot last forever, either," Shadow said. "More than just raiders have come through the Wall. There have been refugees as well. They come to the Star Brethren for succour—they know us from ages past. And they tell us of inner rifts, of rebellions and civil war in far-off provinces, and of an Emperor drawn so thin by centuries of magic-held life that he is hardly even human anymore. The Empire is overcrowded with land-hungry lords and ambitious magicians, and riven with internal strife. It is united only because the Wall is crumbling and there is the prospect of land and booty. Should the Wall be rebuilt . . ."

"They'll turn back on themselves," Rand said fiercely. "The Empire will rip itself apart!"

"It may," Shadow said. "Even if it does not, we will at least have kept the light of peace shining in the Heartland for a time longer. But remember, Prince Rand, like the Empire, the Heartland, too, cannot last forever." He spread his hands. "That is why we are called the Star Brethren. Night approaches, always. It may arrive early or late, but it will come. We hope only to hold it off as long as possible, and perhaps, when it comes, to keep some light shining."

"Then why not give up? If you believe everything you do is, in the end, hopeless . . ."

"There is always hope," Shadow said. "And whatever may happen in the future, we can deal only with the present, and do our best. The One can ask no more of us." Shadow looked into the forest again. "The Unicorn is travelling away from us, southwest. Are you sure . . .?"

"Not until tomorrow," the Prince said firmly, and returned to his injured horse.

In the morning, the animal proved able to carry a rider. Rand would have preferred to let it rest another day, but they dared not let the boys' trail get too cold. Shadow could tell him the Unicorn's general direction, but couldn't pinpoint its location. If they lost the trail, they might spend days trying to find it again—and they didn't have days.

As the Prince rode at a walking pace, Shadow strode alongside. "He's heading home," the Star Brother said suddenly. "Why didn't I realize—"

"Where's home?" the Prince asked.

"Somewhere along the coast . . . in sight of the Wall."

"The Blood Empire has been destroying the villages closest to the Wall," the Prince said grimly.

"I know."

They pressed on in silence.

Around noon, they came to a hollow where a man lay stretched out on the ground by the cold ashes of a fire. The Prince dismounted and signalled Shadow to stay put, then slowly crept through the trees toward the motionless figure. But when he got close enough to see the man clearly, he stood up abruptly and called Shadow to him.

Together they examined the stiffened corpse, which stared at the sky with glazed eyes. "There's not a mark on him," the Prince said. "What killed him?"

"The Unicorn," Shadow said grimly. "Just as it killed the Empire agent who tried to steal it from Gondwain."

Rand looked at the pain etched on the corpse's face. "What must this boy be suffering, carrying such a thing?"

"More power has been drawn from the Unicorn," Shadow said. "We may be running out of time."

The Prince didn't reply. He stared into the dark forest.

Like a hunted animal fleeing to its den, Nels was heading blindly for home, cursed with a deadly magical artifact, pursued by a terrifying foe . . . and carrying the fate of the Heartland in his young hands.

Rand only hoped he found the boy before that fate—and Nels's—was sealed.

CHAPTER 12
A WARM WELCOME

Full night descended before Nels and Dart reached the solitary house above the bay, the starlight too dim for them to see more than that it was low and rambling. Yellow light shone through the score of small round panes in the two fine glass windows on either side of the front door, and an inviting odour of woodsmoke and roasting meat hung in the air.

Dart paused at the edge of the yard, sniffing that good smell suspiciously. "You're sure this house wasn't here when you left?"

"Of course I'm sure." Brushing past her, Nels stepped into the clearing, a strange warmth momentarily suffusing his chest from the unicorn. He ignored it—it had been glowing off and on ever since they came to the village— and strode forward.

"Looks like it's been here a hundred years," Dart muttered behind him, but she followed.

Nels pounded on the front door with his fist. At once they heard footsteps inside, and a moment later the door swung open.

A tall man wearing a long grey robe, sashed with red, looked down at them. A broad smile spread across his fine-featured face. "My word! Guests! Come in, lads, come in! I get few visitors out here!"

Nels, expecting a cautious fisherman terrified by the destruction of the village, found himself standing in the wood-panelled entrance hall with Dart almost before he knew it. Their host stashed their packs and cloaks in a closet, then ushered them into the living room, seating them in plush red-velvet chairs by the fire crackling merrily in the giant stone hearth, its snaps and pops echoed by a loudly ticking clock on the mantel. "I'm just cooking my supper," he said when they were comfortable. "You must stay and eat with me!"

"If it's no trouble . . ." Nels began.

"Trouble? Not at all. I insist!"

As their host went down another hall toward the kitchen, Nels settled back in the chair, exhausted, all the miles of walking and the shock of finding the village destroyed suddenly hitting him full-force. The fire, the cozy chairs, the thick fur rug under his feet, all promised peace and comfort and rest, at least for a little time. He closed his eyes in contentment . . .

. . . only to be jerked back from the edge of sleep by Dart's hand on his arm, insistently shaking him. "Something's not right here!"

Nels blinked at her. "What?"

"You may trust each other out here, but nobody can be as trusting as he's pretending to be. He hasn't even asked our names, much less what we want or why we're here. He didn't even peek first to see what we looked like before he opened his door to us. And I'm supposed to believe this man has just seen magic blast his village to nothing?"

"Oh, thank the One for your good fortune and relax!" Nels snapped. "We were supposed to spend tonight in my home. It's gone. Would you rather sleep in the woods again?"

Dart stood up abruptly. "Maybe I would!" She stalked back to her chair.

Their host returned with platters of meat and vegetables and steaming mugs of berry tea. Dart's doubts, Nels noted, had not affected her appetite.

Throughout the meal, their host chattered about inconsequential things, the weather, the shocking decline in the local game population, even how poor the fishing had been, but he never mentioned the ruined village or the Blood Empire—or explained who he was or why he lived all alone, miles from anywhere.

Weary to his bones, Nels wanted only to enjoy the fire, the food and that marvellous chair. But Dart had planted a seed of doubt in his mind, and finally, he tried to steer the conversation toward some of the questions that needed answers. "Isn't there a village near here?" he began innocently. "That's what we were looking for when we stumbled on your house, but we couldn't see any lights along the coast . . ."

Their host laughed. "I wondered how long it would take you to get to that." He rose from his chair and wandered casually to the window behind Dart's chair. "I would have explained things earlier, but I didn't want to spoil your meal." He turned to face Nels. "I wanted you well-fed for the long journey ahead of us."

Nels stared at him. "What are you talking about?"

"My dear boy, haven't you figured it out yet?" Suddenly, the entire room wavered, like a reflection in a wind-troubled pool, and the genteel man in the grey cloak vanished, replaced by an armoured figure wearing a red tunic and cloak, eyes glinting through the eyeslits of his helmet. "You are coming with me to my Emperor."

Nels grabbed for the unicorn, but the Horseman seized Dart's shoulders, pinning her to the chair. "Touch the Dark Unicorn and he dies!" He looked down, then back to Nels. "No," he said, his voice a low, purring growl. "I sense the truth. *She* dies."

Dart sat like stone under his touch, her eyes wide with either fear or—more likely, knowing Dart—blazing anger.

"Leave her alone!"

The Horseman's mailed fingers tightened, and Dart winced. "Will you come with me to the Emperor?"

Nels hesitated, and the gauntleted hands tightened again. Dart cried out, squirming uselessly. "All right! I'll come!" Nels said hastily.

The Horseman loosened his grip on Dart, but didn't

release her. "Very good. I suggest you rest now. I prepared a guest room for you down the hall. We head south at first light."

"What about Dart?" Nels demanded.

"She stays here, where I can watch her. And lest you have foolish thoughts of escape, I warn you: I do not sleep."

"Then I stay here, too!"

The Horseman shrugged. "As you wish." He finally let go of Dart's shoulders, but remained standing behind her chair, arms folded.

The clock on the mantle ticked on relentlessly through the night, each tick an eternity. Exhaustion would weigh down Nels's eyelids, but every pop of the fire or creak of the house's beams in the cold night air would jerk him awake again, and always, the Horseman stood unmoving. Nels had thought the burning glint in his eyes to be a reflection of the fire, but as the fire slowly died, that glint grew brighter.

Dart's eyes were closed, but watching the rapid rise and fall of her chest, Nels doubted she slept any more than he did.

The Horseman feared the unicorn—the Dark Unicorn, he had called it—that much seemed obvious. But Nels, even if he could have touched it with the Horseman watching him, didn't know how to use its power against him. Before it had protected him when he was directly attacked, but how to use it to protect someone else . . .

He suspected the Horseman knew; obviously, those

who were after the unicorn knew exactly what it was, whereas he knew only the frightening things it had done since he unwittingly "inherited" it.

Those who were after the unicorn . . . Something the Horseman had said suddenly registered on him. They were to ride *south*! And he had called his master "the Emperor." The Horseman served not King Athelras, as Nels had assumed, but . . .

The Blood Empire, he thought in mingled horror and disbelief.

Could the Emperor have destroyed his village just to bait the trap into which he and Dart had fallen? He knew the answer before he asked the question; of course, he could. He must have. He knew that when Nels found his home destroyed, and then saw a light in the hills above it, he would have to approach it to find out what had happened.

All that destruction, all those deaths, just to get him and the unicorn . . . just what *did* hang around his neck?

Whatever it was, how could it be worth all this suffering?

It couldn't. It *couldn't*. And at that moment, if he could have seized it, he would have thrown it into the fire . . .

. . . except, of course, he thought grimly, it wouldn't let him.

A grey, cloudy morning came at last. The wind, whipping in from the sea, howled in the eaves. As the first unhappy light of dawn crept in through the shutters, the

Horseman suddenly stirred. "Up, you two!" he snapped. "The Emperor awaits. Boy, get the packs."

Nels obeyed. In a few moments, the three of them were outside and striding south through the trees. Through a gap to their right, Nels glimpsed the village one last time, its ruins forlorn and desolate in the wintry light.

He glanced back at the cottage and stopped so suddenly that Dart ran into him. Grey, tumble-down walls, no roof—ruins fifty years old, at least. No wonder the unicorn had flashed with warmth as he approached the cottage—and the more fool he for ignoring it. Had even the food been an illusion?

His stomach rumbled with hunger. Perhaps it had.

"Quit lagging, boy!" The Horseman gave him a push that sent him stumbling, and, furious at his own stupidity, he didn't look back again.

They hadn't gone far when the Horseman's fiery black stallion, already bridled and saddled, came galloping through the trees, puffing clouds of breath like white smoke in the icy air. The Horseman mounted with practised ease and swung Dart roughly up in front of him. "You walk," he told Nels. "I want the girl up here where I can control her—and you."

The unicorn must have the power to free them both, Nels thought bitterly—and he couldn't use it. And what if he tried, and something went wrong? He remembered the horrible death of the robber on the trail. That could be Dart.

He couldn't even be certain that the unicorn could destroy the Horseman. Those eyes . . . whatever lurked inside that closed helmet, Nels thought, might not even be human—at least not entirely.

"Faster, boy!" the Horseman ordered. "We must reach the Wall before dark!"

This is what the weakening of the Wall means, Nels thought grimly. *The likes of* him *free to ride into the Heartland. Dart said there were rumours in Koroth . . . King Athelras must know. I wonder what he's doing about it?*

Probably massing the Heartland's army, if "massing" could be applied to the pitiful number of soldiers the Heartland, at peace for decades, could muster. And only a few miles from here, the Blood Empire must already have its hordes in position along the Wall, ready to sweep through the Heartland. He knew from the history his father had taught him that unless the Empire had shrivelled in a thousand years, the Heartland, poorly armed and completely without magic, could not hope to survive.

The Empire has won the war without even fighting it, he thought. *Why do they need me?*

And then another thought struck him. The Horseman rode for the Blood Emperor, not Athelras, but Athelras, too, must know of the unicorn's power. The Empire might want it, but the Heartland *needed* it. Why hadn't he and Dart seen anything of Athelras's men?

He thought of the strange things Shadow had told him, and of the dying man who had given him the unicorn, and suddenly, a lot of things fell into place. Shadow and the dying man had both been serving Athelras. The Empire had already been after it, had almost captured it at the bridge in Nimgar. Instead, it had fallen to Nels, and then, when he could have delivered the unicorn to Athelras himself in Koroth, he had instead assumed that Athelras was the enemy and had fled the city, possibly taking with him the one hope the Heartland had of standing against the Blood Empire.

And now, helplessly, he would deliver the unicorn to the Emperor with his own hands. *It would be best for everyone if I threw myself off the nearest cliff!* he thought savagely, but knew that even that would not absolve him. If anything happened to him, the Horseman would have no more reason to keep Dart alive. His death would mean her death, too.

And he didn't want to die—he wanted to fight the Horseman and everyone like him!

His thoughts were shattered by the Horseman's boot as the rider kicked him savagely to the ground. A moment later, Dart fell beside him.

As they struggled to their feet, they saw the Horseman draw his sword, an eerie blade blazing with blue fire, and rein his steed sharply around to face another armoured man thundering toward them on a white warhorse, his own sword whirling over his head.

CHAPTER 13
SWORD TO SWORD

As Prince Rand and Shadow tracked the boys through the afternoon, Rand became more and more convinced Shadow had guessed right: Nels was heading home. "I've studied battle maps of all this terrain," Rand finally said. "If we don't try to follow Nels's exact path, I think I can save us several hours—enough that we might be able to catch them before they get dangerously close to the Wall." He held out his hand to Shadow. "My horse will carry us both."

"He's been injured," Shadow protested. "I can walk . . ."

"Not as fast as he can, even double-mounted."

"But . . ."

"Don't argue with your prince."

Shadow sighed. "No, my lord," he said, and took the proffered hand.

On a cold, grey morning three days later, they stood

beside the Prince's horse, looking down at the blasted ruins of the village that had been Nels's home.

"This was more than a random attack, I'll wager," Shadow said, his face grim. "No mere raiding party did this."

"Could the boy have been here?" Rand asked.

"No," Shadow said flatly. "If he had been, the Dark Unicorn would lie below, and it does not." His gaze slowly travelled the slopes above the ruined village. "But it is near . . . I feel it!"

The Prince turned back to his mount. "They wouldn't have stayed down there. They had to have climbed out some—"

"The Red Horseman!" Shadow suddenly cried.

"What?" Rand stared around. "Where?"

"There!" Shadow pointed to a gap in the trees above the village, but Rand saw nothing.

"You're sure?"

"Of course I'm sure!"

"The boys?"

"One of them, at least."

Rand swung into his saddle. "He's taking them to the Emperor! Follow on foot!" He spurred his horse to a gallop.

"Go with the One!" Shadow cried after him.

Ravines and slippery slopes and tangled undergrowth slowed his headlong pace around the bay, but whenever the footing improved he urged the stallion on again, and at last he reached the spot where Shadow had seen the

Horseman, and reined to a sudden halt beside a ruined cottage—a ruin with smoke still rising from the coals of a fire in the shattered fireplace.

He dismounted and searched the ground, and almost at once saw the familiar footprints he had trailed for so long, but mingled with the deeper marks of steel-shod feet. Rand looked at the ruined cottage and thought he knew what must have happened. The boys would have been shocked and horrified at what had happened to the village; seeing a light on the hill above, of course, they would have gone to it to find out what had happened. They'd delivered themselves to the Red Horseman without his having to lift a finger.

With an oath, Rand leaped astride his mount and galloped after them.

A short distance beyond the house, the tracks changed. The Horseman and one of the boys had mounted, but one boy remained on foot, which gave Rand hope. If his quarry moved no faster than a walking boy, he still had a chance to catch them before they reached the Wall.

As he galloped, he felt the first uncertainty in his stallion's gait, as though the horse were once more favouring, ever-so-slightly, the injured leg. But he didn't let up, though the lameness grew worse, and every stride stabbed his own heart with pain. He promised to make it up with extra oats and two weeks' rest, and plunged his heels into the stallion's flanks again.

At last, he glimpsed the Horseman ahead, one boy in

the saddle in front of him, the other walking with his hand on the stallion's bridle.

He tried to spur his mount to even greater speed, but the horse had no more to give; Rand drew his sword and whirled it over his head.

The Horseman kicked one boy to the ground, then threw the other from his saddle and spun to meet the Prince with a sword that dripped blue fire.

Rand almost laughed. No sword or sword arm could stop a stroke with the momentum his would carry.

But at the last instant, his stallion failed him. The injured leg buckled and the horse fell, and the stroke that should have shattered both the Horseman's sword and the Horseman's arm clanged uselessly off the blue blade, with a flash like summer lightning . . . and Rand, thrown from the saddle, crashed into the Horseman, sending both of them thudding to the ground.

The Horseman's sword flew from his grasp, but Rand, stunned by the blue backlash of the Horseman's blade and by the force of his fall, couldn't muster the energy to rise, much less strike the Horseman, even though the armoured figure lay quiescent under him.

Quiescent only for a moment: the Horseman suddenly stiffened and hurled him away. He crashed face-first into the ground, spat blood and grass from his mouth, and looked blearily up to see the Horseman staggering to his feet.

With muscles that didn't want to work properly, he pushed himself upright, casting around for his sword. He didn't see it—but the Horseman's blade, no longer ablaze, lay only inches away.

The Horseman saw it too and stumbled toward it, but with painful effort, Rand scrabbled for it and managed to get his hand on the hilt. At once, the blue flames licked around the blade again. Swaying, he rose to his knees and pointed the sword at the Horseman, who stopped a few feet away.

"The boys are gone," Rand croaked. "You have failed."

"You do not have the Dark Unicorn, either," the Horseman growled. "There is still time."

"They know what you are, now. You will not trap them again."

The Horseman stepped forward. "Give me my sword."

"With pleasure." Though the world whirled around him, Rand got one foot under him, then the other. "Come closer and receive it!" He levelled the strange weapon at the Horseman's heart. The servant of the Blood Empire backed slowly away; then, with lightning quickness, leaped astride his black steed and galloped out of the clearing.

Rand's last strength vanished with his foe, and as he crumpled to the ground, the flame of the magical sword went out.

CHAPTER 14
ON THE RUN AGAIN

Nels stared at the strange rider galloping toward them, but Dart, as soon as she had scrambled back to her feet, grabbed his arm and pulled him into the woods.

Behind them, steel clashed once, with overtones of thunder, and a brilliant, lightning-like flash momentarily cast the trunks of the trees into stark relief, but Dart didn't look back. "Killed each other, more'n likely," she panted. "Blazes, Nels, can't you run any faster?"

"If they're both dead . . .

"Well, maybe they're not. Maybe that Red Horseman will be after us again in a minute. And if he's not riding after us, maybe the man who killed him is. Are you sure you want him to catch us, either?"

Well, when she put it that way . . . Nels put a little more kick into his stride.

Dart kept angling slightly to one side or the other,

confusing their trail, and when both of them were trotting more than running and sucking in air in huge, painful gasps, she finally halted. "Now . . . we use . . . our heads," she panted. "This way." She led Nels into a thicket of brambles that stabbed through cloth and sometimes skin, so dense that twice he thought he'd stick fast and have to wait for the Horseman or his attacker to come cut him out. But finally they emerged, scratched, breathless, and sweating, on the other side, and Dart looked back with satisfaction. "I'd like to see the horse that could come through that!"

Nels sat gratefully on a fallen log. "I don't think anyone came after us."

Dart sat beside him. "Maybe not yet, but they will. One or the other."

"That could have been a rescue!"

"Or someone worse than the Red Horseman."

"We should have stayed and found out."

"Blazes, Nels, he was probably somebody else from the Blood Empire wanting the glory of bringing you in—or a robber who didn't know who we were but figured we must be worth something."

Nels stood and looked back the way they had come, though a mile of forest now hid the clearing where the battle had taken place. "I've been wondering why we haven't seen anything of Athelras's men. Maybe that was one. We should go back . . ."

Dart pulled him down again. "You listen to me!" she snapped. "You're new at this, but I've been running for my life *all* my life. The number-one rule of survival is run first, ask questions later. The number-two rule is *don't* ask questions later. The less you stick your nose into things that don't concern you, the longer you'll keep it. And the number-three rule of survival is look out for yourself, because nobody else is going to do it for you. And if you think someone *is*, don't trust them!"

Nels threw her hand off and stood. "No wonder you've always been alone." He turned his back on her and began pushing through the brambles.

He heard her behind him, but was too busy avoiding nettles to look back. When at last they emerged from the thicket, she grabbed his shoulder and spun him around. "You go back there and you're marching yourself and that demon-blasted unicorn right into the Blood Emperor's clutches!"

Nels jerked free and strode on, fallen leaves swirling around his boots. "We don't know that. Maybe the man who attacked the Horseman is here to take us back to our own king . . ."

"Oh, that would be wonderful, wouldn't it? Noble King Athelras?" Dart ran in front of him and stopped him with a hand on his chest. "You think that would be any better?"

Nels pushed her hand away again. "The unicorn has power. If the Wall is crumbling, the Heartland needs that power."

Dart grabbed both his arms. "Which means he wasn't rescuing us, he was rescuing the unicorn!" He tried to shrug free, but she wouldn't let him go. "Will you listen to me? Athelras and his Guard are no better than the Blood Emperor and the Horseman as far as the likes of you and me are concerned! They'll use you, then throw you away like a worn-out shoe!"

"You would feel that way, wouldn't you?" Nels snapped, then immediately wished he hadn't.

"Because I'm a thief?" Dart's cheeks flamed red. "So I've got something to worry about, and you don't? You bloody —yes, damn you, I was a thief—the best! And some choice I had!"

Nels remembered what she had told him, why she had left her "family" to become a thief in the first place, and felt lower than a maggot.

"Your noble Athelras hasn't done me a precious lot of good, has he? Why should I help him?"

"Look, Dart, I understand how you feel—"

"Like hell you do!"

"—but I have to know. If someone else is after me, I have to know who and why. And if it was someone who can help us . . ."

"Blazes!" Dart let go of his arms. "All right! Let's go! But don't say you weren't warned!"

Her capitulation was so sudden that despite her release of his arms, Nels didn't move. "Wait a minute. You've agreed?"

"No, I haven't agreed! But I'm not going to convince you, am I, and I'm not going to let you go back by yourself. So quit wasting time."

Nels looked at her scowling face and half-smiled. "Thank you."

"Shut up and start walking."

Feeling warmer than the cold wind should have permitted, Nels obeyed.

He did heed Dart's warning enough to slow his pace and try to remain hidden as they neared the clearing. He could hear nothing but the wind in the trees; the battle seemed to be over.

"Both gone?" he whispered to Dart.

"Or dead."

"Cheerful as usual." He crept closer, until, pushing the barren branches of a bush to one side, he could finally see the clearing.

The white horse that the Red Horseman's attacker had ridden grazed on the sparse brown grass on the other side of the clearing, favouring its left foreleg. Its rider lay crumpled in his grey cloak at the centre of the field, just visible in the long grass. The Red Horseman and his black steed had vanished.

Nels cautiously stepped out into the field, half-expecting the Red Horseman to come galloping out of the forest.

But nothing of the sort happened, and a moment later, he and Dart knelt beside the fallen man.

They turned him over, searching for a wound, but found nothing. "He's alive, but barely breathing," Dart said. "What happened to him?"

"Could he have been knocked off his horse?"

"Maybe . . . but why didn't the Red Horseman kill him?"

Nels couldn't answer that. He reached out to touch the hilt of the sword that lay beside the unconscious man, but snatched his fingers back as blue light ran the length of the blade. "That's the Horseman's sword!"

"But where is he?" Dart stood up and slowly turned, surveying the clearing.

Nels stood, too. "Driven off, I guess."

"Then he'll be back, either to get his sword or look for us. And our friend here . . . if he *is* our friend . . . isn't going to be able to protect us."

"We should help him," Nels said, looking down at the fallen man again.

"Nels, much as I admire your desire to do the right thing, staying here until the Red Horseman returns is not going to do this fellow a hell of a lot of good, is it?"

"No, but . . ."

"But, nothing." She spread the man's cloak over him, then took a blanket from her own pack and added that. "There. He won't freeze. It looks to me like he's been stunned. He'll probably wake up none the worse."

"But I need to talk to him!"

"We can't wait that long." Hands on her hips, she glared at him. "I gave in once. But that's it. We have to run while we've got the chance. The more miles we can put between ourselves and the last place the Horseman saw us, the better chance we have to get away clean."

Nels looked around at the woods again, suddenly feeling very exposed. "You're right. Let's get out of here."

"With pleasure!"

Dart led the way out of the clearing, taking a different direction than when they had first fled. "I'm confusing the trail," she explained tersely.

"I thought you grew up in the city."

"The principle's the same." She gave him a rare smile. "Just don't ask me to live off the land. If it doesn't walk on two legs and carry a jingling purse, I don't know how to hunt it!"

They continued through the afternoon in a generally easterly direction, pausing only to rest and to refill their canteens at a swift, clear stream. At least they didn't have to worry about losing their sense of direction, Nels thought, not with the Wall towering like a permanent storm cloud to their right.

As the short autumn day drew to a close, they stopped in a hollow where a tiny spring filled a pool in a mossy circle of rocks. Nels built a fire, and after a meagre supper taken from what little remained of their stores (Dart had stopped complaining about summer sausage, Nels noted), they huddled close together near the flames, their backs against a tree.

"We have to decide where to go," Dart finally said. She moved a little closer to Nels, so that their shoulders touched, adding a little extra warmth.

"I don't know." Nels tossed a stick into the fire with

his. "I can't look for my family, if they're still alive—not with the Horseman after me, and probably Athelras's men, too."

"We can't hide in the forest forever. Our food's almost gone."

"Maybe Strom would take me back," Nels said, then laughed a little bitterly. "Actually, I'm sure he would—to sell me to the highest bidder."

"That just leaves Koroth," Dart said slowly.

Nels looked down into her eyes, only a few inches from his own. "Koroth? The whole city must be alive with guards looking for me."

"Not any more. They know you're gone. And Koroth is my territory; I can hide you forever. With a little more warning, we wouldn't have had to run last time. I even know people who can make you look like someone else. We'd be safe."

Nels looked south. Even in the dark, he could sense the Wall, somehow blacker than even the cloud-shrouded night sky. "If the Wall is crumbling, nowhere is safe," he said softly.

"You don't know the Wall is crumbling."

But Nels felt the strange warmth of the unicorn against his skin and raised one hand to it. "The Red Horseman couldn't have got through if the Wall wasn't weakening. And the unicorn has something to do with it."

Dart snuggled closer to him, and he put his arm around her, his heart suddenly beating faster. "Blast magic," she said. "I wish you'd never found the bloody thing."

"In which case I wouldn't have met you, my *boy*." Nels looked down at her firelit face. "What would your fellow cutpurses say if they saw you now?"

"They can say what they like when we get back."

"You think I'm going to agree with you, don't you?"

"I'm sure of it."

Nels bit his lip. "Well, you're right. Almost."

Dart's eyes narrowed. "Almost?"

"I'll come with you to Koroth. But then I'm turning this thing over to Athelras."

"After all I've told you?" Dart threw his arm from her shoulders.

It suddenly felt much colder. Nel reached out to her. "Dart, I . . ."

"Oh, go to sleep! Blazes!" She leaped up and stalked into the woods, returning a few minutes later only to wrap herself in her blanket and lie down on the far side of the fire, her back to him.

Nels stretched out in his own blanket, missing the warmth of her body next to his as she had snuggled against him beside the tree. Dart would stay with him—she'd proven that earlier, when she'd returned with him to the clearing. She would stay.

Wouldn't she?

But even if she left him, he knew he had to take the Dark Unicorn to Athelras. He'd had a taste of the Blood

Empire; he'd give his own king his chance. Assuming the Red Horseman didn't catch them before they ever reached Koroth.

When at last he slept, the distant thunder of galloping hooves filled his dreams.

CHAPTER 15

THE ONLY HOPE

Rand woke—not easily, as on a sunny morning with the sun shining into his chamber, but all at once, uncomfortably. He jerked upright and almost collided with Shadow, who was bending over him anxiously.

"Easy, my lord," Shadow murmured, trying to push him down. "You shouldn't move so quickly after being unconscious . . ."

"Where are they?" Rand brushed Shadow's hands aside and stared around the clearing, dim in the fading light. His horse raised its head from the long grass and glanced at him, then went back to feeding.

"Where are who?"

"The boys!"

"You've seen them?"

Rand threw off the blanket that covered him and scrambled to his feet. "Of course I've seen them! I . . ." He swayed and sank to his knees again as dizziness claimed him. "I rescued them," he finished weakly.

"You were alone when I found you. What happened?"

The Prince sat down again and told Shadow of his brief battle with the Red Horseman. "The Horseman fled west, the boys east," Rand finished. "I thought they would come back here . . ."

"Maybe they did," Shadow said. "I did not spread that blanket over you."

"Then they did come back!" He stared around at the dark forest again. "But why didn't they stay?"

"They must have feared the Horseman's return." Shadow looked east. "If they fled inland, they won't soon find shelter. I don't think there's a village or farm left this close to the Wall that the Empire hasn't destroyed—and not just by magical fire from the heavens, either. Other things besides the Red Horseman have been coming through the Wall."

"Would other servants of the Empire know about the Unicorn?"

"They will soon, if they don't yet. I'd wager the Horseman has fled back through the Wall to report to the Emperor—and by magical means, the Emperor can contact all of his armies and agents the length of the border in minutes. All of them will be looking for Nels by now." He glanced at the Prince. "And the Horseman will undoubtedly return to take up the chase himself, with the added incentive of desiring to make an end of you, my lord."

"He could have made an end of me this time, had he not fled so quickly," the Prince said ruefully, rubbing his temples.

"He feared his own sword," Shadow said. He bent down and examined the Horseman's weapon without touching it. "Blades like this are mentioned in the ancient tales. Even in the days of magic, they were very rare and powerful. That first contact with it would have killed you if magic were not still weak on this side of the Wall. If the Dark Unicorn hadn't been near, I doubt it would have held even as much power as it did."

"It was enough." The Prince picked up the sword and watched the strange flames lick around its blade. "But I think you're right. The blue glow was much brighter when I fought the Horseman."

"That surge will have drained the Unicorn still more," Shadow said. "It may already be useless to us."

The Prince fingered the blanket. Nels must have been terrified, but he'd still come back to check on the Prince . . . with no way of knowing whether Rand was friend or foe. "The Unicorn seems less and less important," Rand murmured. He looked up. "My horse has reinjured his leg, but I must have him. I dare not ride double, but I must ride."

Shadow inclined his head. "I understand. I will bear word of what has happened back to Koroth . . . if the Wall does not collapse before I can complete the journey."

"Is there anything else of use you can tell me about the Dark Unicorn?"

Shadow sighed. "We know so little . . . I think not, though who knows what forgotten bit of legend or rhyme may prove vital?"

"Do you know how Gondwain triggered the Unicorn? If I do reach Nels, what do I tell him to do?"

His companion spread his hands. "No one knows."

"No one knows!" The Prince stared at him, shocked. "Has this quest been in vain from the beginning, then?"

"No! The power is there. But no one knows how to bring it out. Nels has to find the key within himself."

"Would destroying the Unicorn stop the decay of the Wall? It still stands strong enough to keep the full force of the Empire out of the Heartland, at least."

Shadow looked shocked. "Destroy the Unicorn?"

"If there's no other way, yes!"

The priest shook his head violently. "No! It cannot be done, not by us."

"Then by whom?"

"There is only a legend . . ."

"A year ago, the Dark Unicorn itself was only a legend! Tell me!"

Shadow took a deep breath. "Very well, my lord. As we imperfectly understand magic, even the most powerful spell has a weakness, and can be broken . . . but the more powerful the spell, the more power needed for its breaking." He paused, as though reluctant to say any more.

"And?" the Prince prompted.

"No one in the Heartland has ever practised magic of that kind."

"But the Empire did?"

"And does."

Something High Priest Sartan had said when he first revealed the discovery of the Dark Unicorn to the King and Prince came back to Rand. "I remember now," he said slowly. "A human sacrifice. Sartan said that's the only way to destroy the Unicorn."

Shadow nodded once, grimly.

"What happens if the Unicorn *is* destroyed?"

"All the magic locked within it will be destroyed at the same time. The Wall will fall. The Empire could invade at will, but within the Heartland, it would find its magic greatly weakened. It would make the invasion that much bloodier."

"On their side."

Shadow nodded, barely visible in the night. "On their side. On our side . . . we cannot stand against them for long, whether they are aided by magic or rely solely on the force of arms. If the Dark Unicorn is lost, we are doomed. If it is destroyed, we are doomed. Its power truly is our only hope."

Rand looked up at the brilliant stars beginning to prick the sky, then to the south, where the eternal storm bank of the Wall blotted them out. "Then all our hopes rest on Nels," he said softly. "And he's fleeing right where he will be in the most danger."

CHAPTER 16

HOWLS IN THE FOREST

In the morning, Nels and Dart headed north, thinking that the quickest way to Koroth would be through the mountains that rose inland from Nels's village, but one look at those soaring, snow-covered granite peaks disabused them of that notion.

"There must be passes," Nels said, staring at that forbidding wall.

"But we don't know where, and we don't have time to look," Dart said. "We have to keep moving."

"But where?"

Dart pointed to the right. "East would seem to be our only choice. Maybe we'll spot some way north in a day or two."

"And maybe we'll end up going all the way to the Desolation," Nels muttered, but began walking toward the rising sun.

Dart stopped him. "Not up here on the ridge. Down in

the valley. We're too visible up here." As they picked their way down the slope, she wondered, "If these mountains are so impassable, why does the Heartland have to worry about the Blood Empire invading?"

"I'm sure the Empire knows where the passes are. And anyway, if the Wall crumbles, it could probably make its own passes with magic."

Dart glanced back at those forbidding, saw-toothed peaks. "Magic, huh? You've got magic. You sure that unicorn thing won't let you fly?"

"I have no idea."

Dart grinned. "Why not jump off a cliff and find out?"

Nels laughed and pushed her playfully downhill. "Only as a last resort."

The previous day's wind had blown the clouds away and then subsided, leaving clear, cold skies. The valley they followed slowly broadened as the sun climbed, until, near noon, they began to come across deserted farms, many of the houses ruined or burned. Eventually, they saw, a mile distant, the blackened remnants of a whole village, blasted like Nels's own. "Where is the Heartland's army?" Nels cried in frustration.

"Chasing snowflakes up north." Dart turned in place, scanning their surroundings. "I don't like this. We should stop travelling during the daytime. We're too exposed."

Nothing moved among the ruins, but Nels still felt uneasy. "I think you're right."

They holed up for the rest of the day in a barn that, though missing much of its roof, at least hadn't been burned. Enough hay remained inside to keep them warm, and they even found some ears of corn that they roasted for supper, lighting their fire in a corner of the stone structure where it could not be seen from the fields.

After nightfall, they cautiously set out again. "Even if we find a road going north, we can't use it," Nels said in a low voice to Dart as they picked their way across a stubbled field torn by the hooves of horses. The uneven ground made the footing treacherous. "The Empire will be watching the passes."

"Well, I've always wanted to see the Desolation," Dart said, and Nels smiled in the dark.

But suddenly, it wasn't dark anymore. An eerie green light flared in the south, flickering like a candle flame, then strengthening and abruptly flashing so brightly that Nels cried out. A green bolt of energy hurtled from the southern horizon to a point in the mountains to the north. Moments later they heard a distant rumble, and a few seconds after that the ground trembled.

"Another village?" Nels asked shakily.

"Or the pass." Dart took his hand in the dark. "Let's keep going."

Fingers linked, they moved on through the night, which suddenly seemed to hold more threat than protection.

Sometime long after midnight, they stopped and huddled together against a stone wall. Nels sensed other buildings around them, but all was silent and dark; he didn't want to risk a fire.

Despite his aching, cold muscles, Nels dozed before morning. He woke to Dart's sudden gasp. He started to ask what was wrong, but his eyes and his mouth opened at the same moment, and he found himself suddenly unable to form the words.

In the growing light, he could see that heir sheltering wall was part of a stable in the courtyard of a fine house that must have belonged to a local noble. Though now in ruins, no mysterious blast from the sky had destroyed it: the attack and defence here had been steel against steel.

Bodies and parts of bodies littered the courtyard, lying in pools of frozen and congealed blood among shattered shields and dropped weapons.

More than half of the bodies were not human.

One lay not ten feet from Nels and Dart. Though about the same size as a man, and roughly man-shaped, its head was a hideous caricature of a man's, with a sharply sloping forehead, heavy-lidded eyes, a broad, misshapen nose, and a thin-lipped mouth full of sharp teeth. Thick, shaggy red fur covered its otherwise naked body.

It still clutched a blood-darkened curved sword in one hand and a round shield in the other, but the shield had done it little good: three arrows protruded from its breast, and a fourth had pierced its left eye.

Nels got to his feet and reached shakily for Dart's hand. She clung to it tightly as she stood. "Let's get out of here."

Gaze flicking from side to side at the carnage, irrationally feeling the dead might rise and come after them,

Nels led Dart out of the courtyard. Only when they were on clean grass again did they run. For the moment, Nels didn't care if the whole world saw them.

Sometime later, out of sight of the blood-soaked courtyard, once more safely hidden among the forest's trees, they halted and stared at each other, breathing hard. "What were those things?" Dart gasped.

"Something of the Blood Empire's," Nels replied. "Will our army have to fight *them*?"

Dart shuddered. "What if there are more around?" She stared at him. "What if they were after *us*?"

Nels swallowed hard. The same thought had occurred to him. "We've just got to stay out of sight."

They stayed put for the rest of the day, but neither of them slept much, and neither even brought up the idea of eating until late afternoon, when they made do with a cold meal—a meal which finished off the rations the caravan master had provided.

"There might be food back at the manor . . ." Nels said unwillingly.

"No! I'm not going back in there. There'll be food at other farms, too."

Nels didn't argue.

But they didn't come across any other farms in the night, and by morning, the fertile valley they'd been following had narrowed into an uninhabited, forested gulch that looked like it had never felt an axe or heard a footfall.

The thickness of the woods, revealed in the first light

of morning, lifted Nels's spirits. "Nothing will find us in here. Nothing will even look!"

"What about food? Fancy eating leaves, do you?"

"There'll be nuts or something. We won't starve."

They stopped and slept for a few hours, then moved on even though it was still light, trusting to the trees to hide them. They did in fact find some edible berries (at least, Nels told Dart they were edible, hoping they were the same kind he was remembering from Gull Rock). "See, I told you we won't starve," he said as he chewed and swallowed the mouth-puckering fruit. "Quit worrying."

Dart made a face. "I'd almost rather starve," she said, but she kept eating.

That night, Nels took out his flute and played for the first time in days, to celebrate their relative safety. But far from making him feel happier, it instead thrust him into melancholy. Every note reminded him of his family, dead or homeless, and of how unlikely it was he would ever see them again. At last, he lowered the flute and simply sat with it in his hands, turning it over slowly, watching the play of firelight along its silver length.

Dart had listened silently and now moved closer to him and put her hand over his. "You'll find them again," she said softly.

Nels pulled the unicorn out of his shirt and held it in the palm of his left hand. As it did constantly now, it glowed dimly orange, radiating the warmth of a living thing. "Not as long as I have this. I used to tell myself nothing could ever come between me and my family, but

—" He clenched the unicorn tightly in his fist. "This was all it took. It may have led to their deaths . . ."

"You don't know that."

"I don't know otherwise, either." Nels opened his hand again. "It's the reason we're running across Empire-infested territory with who-knows-what looking for us. I hate the thing, Dart . . . but I can't get rid of it. I can't even make the motion of throwing it away. It *owns* me." He let it drop. "It may be worth a kingdom, but it's no replacement for my family."

"At least you're not alone." Dart's eyes met his. "You have me."

And then she leaned forward and kissed him on the mouth.

Before he could respond, she jerked back and stared around at the woods. "What was that?"

Nels, heart pounding, had to swallow before he could speak. "I didn't hear anything."

"Listen! There it is again!"

Very faintly, Nels heard a distant, high-pitched wail. "A night-bird," he suggested, though goosebumps had erupted up his arms and down his neck. "I think it's gone."

But the sound came again, louder and closer. "Blazes!" Dart leaped up and strode to the side of the clearing closest to the sound. "What if it's one of those *things*?"

The wail came again, and again seemed just a little nearer.

Nels joined her. "It's probably nothing to do with us. This is a forest—it has wild animals."

"All the same . . ."

"Come back to the fire." Nels led her back. "We probably won't even hear it again."

Nels's thoughts were more on that brief kiss than on the strange sound, but the moment had passed. Dart rolled herself in her blanket, positioning herself so she could watch the forest in the direction from which that strange call had come.

Nels sat by the fire a while longer, staring into the flames. Dart's kiss had brought to the forefront feelings he'd hardly realized he had. He'd thought of Dart as a boy for days, hadn't even been certain he could call "him" a friend. And since he'd found out—in such embarrassing fashion—that "he" was a she, Dart had gone out of her way to prove she didn't need anybody looking after her, that she was every bit as capable as he was. He snorted. *More* capable, to be perfectly honest with himself. If he'd listened to her when they'd entered the Red Horseman's cottage . . .

She'd proved she really was his friend when she'd agreed to return with him to the clearing where the Red Horseman had been attacked. But that kiss had suddenly made him realize that friendship wasn't a strong enough word for his feelings toward her.

Finally, Nels lay down, too. Though he heard that chilling call from the depths of the woods once more, it wasn't that that kept him awake long into the night.

"I don't care how safe you think we are, if we're still in these woods tonight, I'm keeping watch," Dart said in the morning, over an unsatisfactory breakfast of berries and cold water drawn from beneath the thin ice covering a nearby stream. "What were you thinking of, going to sleep?"

"You were asleep, too!" Nels protested.

"Yes, but I lay down first. I assumed you'd keep watch and wake me when it was my turn. I'm lucky I woke up at all!"

"But there wasn't anything to be afraid of!" Nels said, his voice rising a bit. "It was just a bird or animal!"

"You didn't know that!" Dart shook her head. "Easy pickings, Nels. That's what you are."

Nels bit off a hot retort and let the matter drop, but as they set out east again, he was having second thoughts about what term he wanted to apply to his relationship with Dart.

Late in the morning, they came to a broad, open area, overgrown with waist-high weeds whose brown stalks rattled like dry bones in a rising wind. "This looks like old farmland," Nels said in astonishment. "Who would have lived out here?"

"Or *what?*" Dart glanced over her shoulder.

Nels carefully looked north and south. "Nothing moving; we should be safe enough."

But as he stepped out into the field, he heard Dart mutter, "That's what you said in the forest."

He might have done a little muttering of his own at that point if his eyes hadn't been drawn to a strange hill directly ahead. Tall trees grew up both slopes, but he

thought he glimpsed something through the branches . . ."
It's a ruin!" he cried, stopping so suddenly that Dart ran into him.

"What is?" she demanded irritably.

"On the hill!" He pointed, then looked down at the lump of the unicorn, tucked under his shirt. "The unicorn is getting warmer. There's magic around."

"Then let's bloody well avoid the ruin! I've had enough magic."

"But what could it be, way out here?" Nels stared intently at the top of the hill, but could only make out a sketchy outline of castle-like walls. "And when was it built? It looks ancient!"

"If you have any hopes of becoming ancient yourself, you'll stay away from it."

Nels turned to argue with her, but before he could say anything, the terrifying wailing of the night before filled the clearing, its source as near as the forest.

There could be no more doubt: something was after them.

CHAPTER 17
THE RUINED CASTLE

"Run!" Nels shouted, grabbing Dart's hand and plunging ahead. "To the ruins—we can hide there!"

Dart held back. "The magic—"

The wailing sounded again. "Would you rather wait for *that?*"

Dart quit arguing and started running.

The horrible howl sounded again. An identical call answered it, then another. "There's a whole pack of them, whatever they are!" Nels cried. He tripped and would have fallen if not for Dart's supporting hand.

They reached the treed, ruin-crowned hill and, almost on their hands and knees, picked their way up the slope through thick brush and scattered rubble, all that remained of the outer defences. Near the top, on a small rocky ledge, they paused and looked back at the clearing.

Dart gasped and pointed. "There! Just coming out of the trees!"

Half a dozen of the red-furred creatures whose bodies had been scattered around the ruined manor emerged into the open, loping along more like animals than men, ugly heads thrown back to sniff the breeze. They howled in unison, the sound raising the hairs on the back of Nels's neck, and ran toward the hill.

Nels and Dart exchanged horrified glances, then turned and started scrambling up the steep slope again. A few minutes later, scratched and gasping, they emerged beneath the walls of the courtyard surrounding the main keep.

The ancient outer wall had tumbled down in a dozen places, allowing easy access to the yard beyond, a once-smooth greensward now choked with weeds and saplings. The circular keep rose above the lower ruins of stables and armouries. It had only one door, several feet off the ground, and only thin slits for windows.

Dart's eyes lit up when she saw it. "If we can get inside that, we can fight them off," she said, letting go of Nels's hand. "Boost me up to the door, then I'll pull you up."

A bone-chilling wail drifted into the courtyard. Nels didn't want Dart to enter the keep first—who knew what might be lurking in there?—but she couldn't boost him, there was no time to argue, and he knew by now it wouldn't do any good anyway. So he just nodded and ran with her to the base of the keep.

He lifted her up, legs straddling his head, then leaned

against the wall while she got her feet under her. Standing on his shoulders, she was just able to get her fingertips over the doorsill, and the rough stone offered her enough footholds for her to scramble the rest of the way. She disappeared from Nels's view, but a tense moment later, a length of rope from her pack came tumbling down, and he tested it and found it secure.

A minute after that, he had joined her, and together they pulled the rope inside. Only then did he look around.

They stood in a small chamber with arrow-slits looking out over the courtyard. At the far end of the room, a rusty steel portcullis stood open. "Whoever built this place really hated unexpected visitors," Nels said.

"My kind of people." Then Dart's eyes suddenly widened as she looked over Nels's shoulder, and he spun to see the first of the red-furred creatures nosing into the courtyard. Dart swore.

The creature looked just like the dead ones they had seen; naked, heavily furred, carrying a curved sword and a small, round shield. It sniffed the air, looking around the courtyard, then suddenly stared straight at the door to the keep. Nels took an involuntary step back. "He's seen us!"

The creature threw back its head and screamed, the sound even more terrifying close-up than it had been in the midnight forest. Nels glimpsed its fellows in the woods beyond the wall, running toward the castle; then the first one charged.

Nels heard Dart's knife whisper from its sheath the moment the creature moved. "It can't reach—" he began, then yelped and fell back from the doorway as the creature cleared the threshold with a single mighty leap.

Its sword whistled through the space where he had been a moment before, but it never got a return stroke; Dart ducked and slashed, and hot blood spattered the floor, steaming in the cold. The creature screamed and fell backward into the courtyard, crashing onto a ruined wall. It twitched once, its sword dropping from its hand to clatter on the rocks, then lay still.

Nels picked himself up shakily. Dart stood in the door wearing a death's-head grin, gripping her dripping dagger in one red hand. "You're next!" she shouted into the courtyard, as another of the creatures came through the shattered wall.

Nels finally drew his own knife, but the new creature took a good look at them, then at his dead companion, and stayed put, waiting for the others to join him.

"They can only attack us one at a time," Dart said. "That means we have a chance of fighting them off. We're just lucky they don't have bows."

"How did you learn to fight like that?"

She shot him a withering glance. "I grew up on the streets of Koroth."

Nels held up his own blade. "Well, I'm glad you learned. I don't know how much good I'll be with this."

"Don't you remember what you told me back at the hot pool?" When Nels gave her a quizzical look, she quoted, "Don't worry, I'll protect you.'"

Nels grimaced. "Sorry."

She grinned at him. "I appreciate the thought, anyway." She turned back to the enemy. There were now three creatures in the courtyard, just watching them. "What are they up to? A siege?"

"Why not?" Nels looked down at the red-furred monstrosities. "We have no food or water. All they have to do is wait. If we even fall asleep at the same time . . ."

Dart shook her head without taking her eyes off the creatures. "No," she said. "No, they won't wait. They want you—or at least that blasted unicorn—too much for that." She glanced at his chest. "What does it tell you now, anyway? You said there was magic up here, but these ruins seem harmless enough."

Nels reached inside his shirt and took out the unicorn, holding it in his hand. "It's getting warmer. And glowing brighter." He frowned. "But we're not moving. That must mean . . ." He raised his head and looked past the creatures into the forest beyond. "Someone else is coming. Someone with power."

"The Horseman?"

"I don't know."

Dart pointed her dagger at the unicorn. "Can you use that thing against our ugly friends?"

Nels held it up between thumb and forefinger, staring at it. "I don't know. It has power—more power than we can imagine—I can feel it. But I don't know how to use it." He dropped it in frustration. "The only times it's released any power, I didn't really have anything to do with it—or at least that's what it felt like. I think it was just protecting itself."

"But it also protected you."

"Maybe. Maybe it would act if one of those things down there was standing over me with a sword at my throat, but I'm not anxious to find out."

"We'll leave that to a last resort. You can try it right after you try jumping out the door to see if the unicorn makes you fly." Dart turned her attention back to the courtyard. "If only we had a bow."

"There might be weapons in the keep!" Nels said suddenly.

"Centuries old. I doubt anything usable would have survived."

"We won't know until we look."

Dart shrugged. "True enough."

Nels hesitated. "I believe a proper gentleman would guard the door while you took a look, but . . ."

"But I'm the one who knows how to use a knife," Dart finished. "Forget being a gentleman. Go see what you can find. Believe me, if they start attacking, you'll hear about it."

Somehow not much reassured, Nels turned and went through the portcullis to the chamber beyond.

The keep had a central stairway opening onto the various levels, with one or two rooms on each level. But the rooms were all empty, stripped of any furnishings and any arms when the fortress was first abandoned or over the years since.

This place must have guarded a pass through the mountains, Nels thought as he combed through it. *Back before the Wall. And once the Wall went up, it served no purpose . . .*

Until now. It was a measure of how slowly the Heartland's army was reacting to the threat of invasion that such a strategic fortress remained abandoned. If only it had been re-garrisoned, they might have a chance.

He continued climbing, checking every room without much hope and even less success, until at last, he came out onto the battlemented roof.

He turned first to the south, toward the black bulk of the Wall, which seemed very close and very solid from this height, though he knew it was at least ten miles away and, as proven by the things in the courtyard, anything but solid anymore.

Then he looked north, toward the mountains that cut them off from the rest of the Heartland, and saw at once a V-shaped cut in the wall of rock, one that could mark the entrance to a pass.

But then he looked around the rooftop itself, frowning. It seemed . . . familiar, as though he'd stood in that very spot before. Ridiculous, of course . . . but the feeling grew stronger. He found himself gripping the unicorn tightly and forced himself to release it, letting it dangle free on the front of his shirt.

Then he blinked. Were his eyes playing tricks on him, or was the rooftop not quite as smooth and unmarked as he had thought?

He knelt, then went to his hands and knees to peer at

the stones. An intricate network of fine, faint, barely visible lines marked the roof, perhaps once more deeply engraved but weathered almost completely away by the passage of time.

Nels knelt even closer, trying to make out the design. As he did so, the unicorn dangling around his neck touched the roof.

Instantly, the engraving flared with light, fire pouring through every line, and Nels yelped and scrambled to his feet.

At once, the engraving began to fade again, but not before he saw it clearly.

A large circle, easily twelve feet in diameter, contained within it a six-pointed star, which contained another circle, which contained a triangle. And glowing in the centre of the triangle . . . a unicorn, rearing, pawing the air, just like the carving warm against Nels's chest.

Nels stared at that fading design. Old tales came back to him, tales of magical patterns drawn with chalk or carved in stone, patterns that channelled wizards' powers and allowed them to call and bind demons to their will.

Was that the source of the Dark Unicorn's power? Demons? Had it been created by one of the Blood Empire's evil sorcerers, and not a hero of the Heartland at all?

But if the unicorn were evil, why did the Heartland want it as badly as the Empire? To destroy it? Or, in desperation, would they turn to evil to fight evil? That way lay ruin, Nels felt sure. Did King Athelras, as Dart kept saying, care only for power, and not for the good of his people?

A rising wind whipped dust across the broad stone roof, hiding the diagram's fine tracing. Black clouds Nels had seen no sign of moments before suddenly swallowed the sun, plunging the rooftop and the surrounding countryside into gloom.

Lightning flashed along the southwestern horizon, and a few seconds later, Nels heard the mutter of thunder. The wind began to howl among the fortress's ruins.

He stared at the approaching storm. Had he summoned it when he accidentally touched the unicorn to the diagram?

The wind screamed louder . . .

Nels stiffened. *That's not the wind!*

He plunged back into the stairwell and clattered dizzyingly down the tightly winding spiral, twice almost falling but catching himself and plunging on. Dart's scream met him again before he was halfway down.

The unicorn grew rapidly warmer and began to glow brighter and brighter, but Nels hardly noticed. At last, he burst into the portcullis chamber—and skidded to a horrified halt. "No!" he screamed.

The Red Horseman stood over Dart with a bloody sword in one hand, his eyes pits of fire in the visor-slit of his helmet. "Yes," he said, and his voice was like the grating of a tomb door swinging closed.

CHAPTER 18

RAND'S WILD RIDE

Rand had hopes of catching the boys quickly, but the first trail he followed from the clearing led him through a heavy stand of thorns, then doubled back to the clearing again. By the time he sorted out the signs and found the true trail, half the morning was gone.

Forced to move slowly in order to follow the somewhat meandering trail, leading his limping horse much of the time, he lost much of the advantage he'd hoped being mounted would give him over the boys. In the afternoon, he came on their camp of the night before, but darkness closed down and forced him to stop before he could move more than a few miles farther east.

He slept uneasily, knowing that ahead lay the region where the Blood Empire's raiders had been most active, and keenly aware of Shadow's prediction that by now all of the Empire's servants on this side of the Wall would know of the boys and what they carried.

He woke in the middle of the night to a distant rumble like thunder, but when he sat up and stared around the horizon, the only sky not pricked with stars was that blotted out by the Wall.

The next morning, he reached torn fields and deserted, ruined farms, and found the barn where the boys had camped at least part of the night or the previous day. He pressed on, thinking he might catch them before sunset, but just before noon, he glimpsed the glint of sunlight on steel and had to hide in the woods while a long column of red-furred monstrosities crossed the fields ahead of him, heading north.

Rand had studied more of the ancient histories after the meeting with Sartan had convinced him of the reality of both magic and the Blood Empire, and so could even put a name to the creatures: *fiend-soldiers,* the warriors of Gondwain's day had called them. The size of the force disturbed Rand, though the fiend-soldiers were not true men and so perhaps could move through the Wall more freely than the Empire's main army, which still seemed to be excluded.

He guessed the fiend-soldiers' goal to be one of the few passes through the Shield Mountains. Such a pass would be the first thing needed by the Blood Empire when the Wall collapsed. Rand knew the Heartland's army should be no more than two days away at the most, and for a moment, watching the fiend-soldiers advance, he wondered if his duty didn't lie more with his father's soldiers than in this wild chase across enemy-held land.

But he thrust the thought away. His success or failure in this "wild chase" meant far more than any contribution his sword-arm might make to the army. The slim hope of victory lay not with force of arms, but with the Dark Unicorn.

He hid that night in a ruined farm, not daring to light a fire, and had to wait until late the next morning to press on because of yet another column of fiend-soldiers. It wasn't until mid-afternoon that the boys' trail led him to a ruined manor.

Horror gripped him when he rode into the courtyard. His eyes flicked from one corpse to another, searching for two that might be his quarry, before he realized this battle-carnage was too old to have involved Nels and his friend. He couldn't imagine them staying long with such unpleasant companions, and, casting around the court-yard, he soon came on their trail and followed it into the woods and from there on eastward.

That night, he woke in the dark to a distant high-pitched wail. Fiend-soldiers on the hunt. But what—or who—were they hunting?

The next day, he found out. A mile farther on, the familiar footprints of the boys, left in a marshy bit of ground, were overlaid by clawed, naked feet. Fiend-soldiers—how many, he could not tell.

The Prince spurred his horse to a gallop, heedless now of its injured leg, leaning low into its wiry, flying mane to avoid the whipping branches of the trees. *What can two boys do against those hell-spawn?* he thought in despair. *If the fiend-soldiers reach them before I do . . .*

The passage of so many through the underbrush had left a trail he couldn't lose. He rode as hard as he dared, but reined to an abrupt halt when, a mile or two past the point where the fiend-soldiers had picked up the boys' trail, he noted signs that another rider had already passed that way.

The Prince knew of only one other horseman who would be following the boys.

Rand rode as if possessed, mercilessly driving his poor host to the best speed it could muster. *The Red Horseman knows now that Nels will never help him,* he thought. *He'll kill Nels, either to take the Unicorn for himself or as the sacrifice needed to destroy it.*

The gloom in the ancient wood deepened, though hours of daylight remained. *Storm coming,* the Prince thought fleetingly.

It broke as he pounded out into a weed-choked meadow. Beyond rose a forested hill, where a single brilliant stroke of lightning outlined a ruined castle against a sky grown black as midnight.

As a scream of terror echoed from the battlemented keep, Rand drew the flickering blue sword he had claimed from the Red Horseman and charged across the meadow.

CHAPTER 19

FOR THE LOVE OF DART

Dart moaned and stirred, and Nels felt weak-kneed with relief. "She's not dead!"

"Not yet," the Horseman grated.

"Don't hurt her!" Nels begged. "I'll do whatever you want!"

"It's too late for that bargain." The Horseman reached down and pulled Dart upright. Her right arm hung limp and dripped blood. "The Emperor's plans have changed."

Nels drew his own dagger, useless though he knew it to be. "What are you doing with her?"

"Do you really think you can stop me with that?" The Horseman held his sword blade close to Dart's throat and began dragging her across the floor toward Nels. "Make a move and she dies now."

Though almost sick with fear, Nels held his ground. "You won't kill her! You want her for something. What?"

"You'll find out—if you live that long!" The Horseman

lashed out with his sword, striking Nels's dagger a blow that numbed his hand and sent the weapon skittering across the floor. It clanged down the stairs behind him. As the Horseman's return strike came slashing back at Nels's throat, he leaped desperately backward.

He lost his footing and crashed down the stone steps. His left arm snapped like a dry branch, his forehead cracked against a sharp edge, and finally, he thudded onto the next landing down with an impact that drove the breath from his body and red-hot skewers of pain into his side, pain that renewed itself with every breath. Dimly, he heard the Horseman climbing the stairs toward the roof, dragging Dart, and with his good arm, he pulled himself around until he faced back up the steps. Blood from his forehead blinding one eye, left arm hanging useless, every breath an agony, he started climbing.

He tried to pull himself upright, but such a wave of dizziness swept over him that he almost fell backward down the steps again. He could only manage a slow crawl, cradling his broken arm close to his body, leaving a smeared trail of blood behind him, step by agonizing step.

The pain increased as his arm, numb at first, began to make itself felt. Twice he had to halt, vision greying, cold sweat drenching him, the first time retching up the sour remnants of his breakfast of berries, the second choking on bile. His world narrowed to the next step, and the next one after that, and the next one after that. He couldn't think of how many he had to climb; each one presented its own near-insurmountable challenge.

He didn't even notice the growing heat of the unicorn.

But at last, a cold blast of wind, laced with icy needles of rain, struck his face. The shock cleared his head somewhat, and he looked up to see the open trap door leading onto the roof only three more steps away. He groped for his dagger, forgetting he had lost it, and found instead the precious silver flute in its pouch on his belt. He pulled out its three pieces and, one-handed, using his chin to hold it in place, clumsily fitted them together; then, holding the instrument like a club, he crawled the last few steps and peered outside.

The darkness of midnight enveloped the rooftop, though somewhere above the pall Nels knew the sun must still shine. The crashing lightning luridly illuminated a scene straight from a nightmare.

The creatures that had been pursuing Nels and Dart stood around the strange engraving . . . and at the centre of that engraving, the Horseman cradled Dart in his arms. As Nels watched, he lowered Dart to the roof and stepped out of the circle.

As blood from Dart's wound touched the engraved stones, the unicorn suddenly flared with energy so intense it scorched Nels's chest like a hot poker laid next to his heart. Gasping, he jerked the chain from his neck, then raised his head to see the Horseman looking straight at him. One of the red-furred monsters looked around and started toward him, growling, but the Horseman stopped him with a harsh command in an unknown language, then spoke to Nels directly. "So, you still live . . . for the moment. Perhaps it is fitting."

"What . . . what are you going to do?" Nels gasped out.

"Destroy the Dark Unicorn, of course." The Horseman gestured at Dart. "You have provided me with the perfect sacrifice."

"Sacrifice?" Horror brought Nels to his feet despite his injuries, though he swayed where he stood. "I won't let you!"

"Will you stop me with that?" The Horseman pointed at the flute, clutched in Nels's right hand. "You can't even stop me with the Dark Unicorn—you don't know how to use it." He shrugged. "But we cannot use it either, since you have linked yourself to it. Therefore, we have decided to destroy it—and with it, all the magic of the Heartland." He laughed harshly. "Perhaps it will comfort you to know that you will die with the Unicorn, so you and your young lover can at least face eternity together!"

He reached down and ripped open Dart's clothes, baring her chest, then placed the point of his sword over her heart as the gathered creatures raised their voices in an eerie, keening wail.

Nels hurled the flute at the Horseman with all his strength, but the Horseman simply flicked his sword up and to the left, and the instrument split against it, clanging away across the roof. "Not good enough," the Horseman said, and lowered the point to Dart's chest once more.

Time seemed frozen around Nels. In his mind, he

envisioned the blade slipping through Dart's white skin, blood fountaining around it . . .

The unicorn's broken chain was still twisted in his fingers. That the unicorn would dissolve and the Wall with it, that he, too, would die, seemed trivial. Clutching the black carving, he lunged forward as the Horseman placed both hands on the pommel of his sword. "No!" he screamed.

He stumbled into the diagram, and suddenly, it blazed again with blood-red fire. Pain exploded in his hand as the unicorn burst into light so brilliant it blinded him even through the flesh of his hand; and then that pain spread through his entire body, setting every nerve aflame, eclipsing the agony of his broken arm. Abruptly, not just the unicorn, but his whole body, blazed with light.

And Nels became . . . more. Still Nels, still full of Nels's memories and fears, but also something stronger and grander and far, far older: Gondwain, he who first used the power of the Dark Unicorn to build the Wall that guarded his precious Heartland, he who had put so much of himself into the artifact.

He knew the Horseman from old, knew the armour hid no living man at all, but a demon bound in human shape by the Emperor's black arts. He knew, too, the foul creatures standing nearby: fiend-soldiers, unnatural, brutish slaves more ape than human.

Dart lay in the very spot where he had stood to create the Wall, pouring so much of his will into the Dark Unicorn that he had ceased to exist except within its heart

—and he knew that if she died with the Horseman's sword through her heart, the Unicorn, the Wall, and the Heartland died with her.

Nels's transformation took only a timeless instant; the Horseman's blade had barely nicked Dart's breast before Nels/Gondwain put forth a fraction of the Unicorn's power and shattered the tempered steel like rotten ice.

The Horseman looked up, and in the widening of his hellfire eyes, Nels/Gondwain saw fear for the first time. He lifted the Unicorn. "No," he shouted, his voice rivalling the near-constant thunder all around. "This shall not be. I call back the power that has gone forth. I call it back to me as I called it to me a thousand years past. I call it to me from every corner of the Heartland. By the love I bear this girl, by the love I bear this land, *the Wall . . . shall . . . not . . . fall!*"

A fiend-soldier raised his sword and fell back screaming, fur ablaze. The others, terrified out of their senses, turned and leaped to their deaths over the battlements. The Horseman took one step back, then two, then dropped to his knees and flung one arm over his helmet's visor as the light pouring out of Nels's body brightened.

In the clearing below, Prince Rand's horse reared, almost throwing him, and he closed his eyes and ducked his head against the brilliance.

In the camp of the Heartland's army, two days' ride north, men leaped up, reaching for their weapons, as the light exploded in the southern sky.

In distant Koroth, Sartan and King Athelras stared out

a tower window and exchanged silent looks of wonder at the false dawn.

From the sea-lapped western coast to the deserts of the Desolation to the ice-bound shores of the north, the Heartland's inhabitants froze, staring at the too-bright sky —and then, the light vanished.

It collapsed back in on Nels like a retreating tide and then burst out again in one direction only, into the vast black Wall, which swallowed every ray.

The Horseman screamed. Something grey and fog-like rose from him and fled southward, leaving behind an empty suit of armour that collapsed, clanging, to the rooftop, the helmet rolling away to stop against the battlements.

For an instant longer, Gondwain looked out through Nels's eyes at Dart's limp form; then he, too, disappeared, leaving only Nels . . . who dropped to his knees and then pitched forward onto his face, the Unicorn dropping from his hand as he reached out with his last bit of conscious- ness for Dart's silent, bleeding body.

CHAPTER 20
TENDING THE WOUNDED

Rand rode into the ruined courtyard of the castle. Overhead, the storm-wrack was breaking up, shafts of sunlight beginning to penetrate the ragged, thinning clouds. At the foot of the keep lay the broken bodies of several fiend-soldiers—but not, praise the One, the bodies of Nels or his companion. Standing in his saddle, Rand pulled himself into the tower—and found himself kneeling in blood.

His heart sank. Two discarded daggers lay nearby. The trail of blood led through the rusted portcullis to the stairs, where more blood, smeared on the steps, led upward to the roof.

And there, at last, Rand caught up with his quarry: Nels, covered with blood, prostrate on the stones, the Unicorn, attached to a broken chain, lying by his open hand, which stretched out toward . . .

Rand blinked. "A girl?"

He knelt beside her, afraid he'd come too late, that the Red Horseman had made his sacrifice, but she still breathed. As for the Horseman . . .

Rand stared at the scattered bits of armour and the red cloak flapping in the still-strong wind. The Horseman gone. The sacrifice still alive. The Dark Unicorn still intact. Rand hardly dared hope, and yet . . .

He turned and looked south. As it had for a thousand years, the Wall stood: black, impenetrable, guarding the Heartland.

"He did it," Rand breathed. "Praise the One, he *did* it!"

But at what cost? Rand knelt beside the fallen youngsters and set to work.

The girl had a small cut above her heart and had lost a lot of blood from a wound in her shoulder, but he thought she would be none the worse for wear in time.

Nels, though . . . he set the broken arm, bandaged the burns and cuts, and bound the broken ribs, but still, Nels lay as though dead, heart barely beating.

Rand carried both of them down to the first chamber at the top level of the tower, where two narrow windows allowed fresh air and at least a little sunlight to penetrate. He covered them with blankets—including the one they had provided him while he lay unconscious in the clearing —and brought up other supplies from his poor, lame horse before going into the forest to gather firewood.

The chamber's hearth proved usable, and he soon had a fire blazing in it. Neither Nels nor the nameless girl stirred through the rest of the day or evening. Rand kept watch on the fire, keeping it burning steadily and occasionally dozing off, his back against the stone wall.

In the morning, the girl moaned a little, then opened her eyes with a gasp. Rand rubbed his eyes—the fire had somehow burned down quite a lot since he'd closed them a moment before to rest them—and went to her. "It's all right, you're safe," he said.

She drew away from him. "Who are you?"

"My name is Rand. Who are *you*?"

"They call me Dart." She squinted up at him. "Wait a minute—I know you—you're the one who attacked the Horseman!" She tried to sit up, but he gently pushed her back. "The Horseman! He hit me with his sword—where is he?"

"Gone. Forever."

"Forever?" She gingerly touched her bandaged shoulder, then winced and jerked her hand back. "Blazes!" Then her glance moved past Rand, and she started up again. "Nels!"

"He's still unconscious." He held her down. "You won't do him any good by standing up and passing out." He took a deep breath. "I'm afraid I don't know anything that would do him any good right now."

"What's wrong with him?"

"Broken arm, broken ribs, some cuts and burns . . . but they're not the problem. It's . . . he should have stirred by now. But he hasn't." He shook his head. "I've seen similar things in injured soldiers. The priests say their spirits have gone somewhere else for a time. We can only hope Nels's spirit comes back."

"He must have saved my life . . ." Dart whispered.

"He saved all our lives. He rebuilt the Wall."

She suddenly threw back her blanket and this time, pushed away the Prince's hands when he would have stopped her from getting up. "Look, you—Rand—you say his spirit is somewhere else. If that's true, we have to try to bring it back."

"We can only wait . . ."

"Maybe. Maybe not." Dart got to her feet, swayed a moment, then crossed to Nels. She knelt beside him and took his hand in hers, pressing it to her breast. "Nels, can you hear me? Come back, Nels. Come back . . ." And then, so low the Prince wasn't even sure he'd heard it, she murmured, "I love you."

Nels didn't stir, but Dart didn't quit. As the day wore on, she never left his side, pausing only to eat and drink a little at the Prince's urging, but otherwise whispering constantly to Nels. When night came, she lay beside him and cradled his head in her arms, murmuring in his ear. The Prince slept and woke in the middle of the night, still hearing that low, reassuring voice.

The next time he woke, to morning twilight, it was to a moan. He raised up, yawning. "Does your shoulder hurt, Dart? I have some herbs that might—"

Dart jerked up, wide-eyed, from where she had fallen asleep beside Nels. "That wasn't me!"

Rand scrambled to Nels and held his hand while Dart

continued to cradle his head. "Nels?" Rand said. "Can you hear us?"

"Nels, wake up!" Dart pleaded. "For me. For your family. Nels!"

The boy's eyes flickered, then opened. He blinked at Rand. "Who are you?" he croaked.

"Nels!" Dart buried her head on his shoulder, crying, sobbing for the first time since Rand had awakened her. Nels held her awkwardly with his one undamaged arm, staring bemusedly at Rand, who beamed down at him.

"Welcome back to the land of the living," said the Prince.

CHAPTER 21

RETURN TO KOROTH

As soon as Nels was able, the three of them moved from the tower and camped in the forest. "It has a cleaner feel," Rand said, and Nels and Dart agreed.

A few days later, they headed north, Rand keeping a slow pace though his horse, thankfully, seemed to have recovered. Nels, though growing stronger daily, still felt very weak, and even riding Rand's horse, while Rand led it, tired him quickly.

As they travelled, Nels told their rescuer the whole story of how he had come into possession of the Dark Unicorn and met Dart, and of their journeys since. Rand said little about himself, except that he was in the service of King Athelras and had tracked them for many days. He listened particularly intently to Nels's story of the disappearance of his family from the destroyed village.

Two days brought them within sight of the Heartland's army, camped at the northern end of the pass through the

Shield Mountains. Rand called a halt, then went on ahead. He came back an hour or so later and told them they had clear passage to Koroth.

By the time the capital city's "shining towers" came into sight five days later, Nels felt much stronger, though his bandaged ribs, arm, and head still bore testimony to his ordeal. Dart, too, had recovered well, except for a stiffness in her arm that Rand assured her would work itself out in time. But as they approached the city, an awkward silence gripped them. "I can't stay here," Nels finally said. "I have to try to find my family."

Dart looked ahead to the walls of the city. "I had a home of sorts here, but no real family," she said softly. "I know that now. I'll come with you."

"Rest with me for a day or two, first," Rand urged. "I'd like you to meet my father."

"But my family . . ." Nels began.

"Another day won't lessen your chances of finding them."

Nels considered. A day or two before setting out on the road again appealed to him—too much to turn down, he decided. "All right."

"Excellent!" Rand had been leading his horse; now he mounted. "I'll ride on ahead and tell my father you're coming. They'll be expecting you at the gate. I'll meet you there." Without giving them a chance to argue, he galloped away.

The city seemed to grow larger very slowly, and the sun touched the western horizon as Nels and Dart finally neared the gate. Deserted wagons and hovels lined the road; the last time Nels had come this way, it had bustled with merchants, peddlers, buyers and beggars—and probably, he thought with a sideways glance at Dart, thieves. "Where is everyone?" he said.

"They must all be inside the walls." Dart looked toward the gate, but nothing moved there, either. "Another festival?"

"It's a quiet one, if it is. Come on." Nels led the way the last few yards.

But before they reached the gate, Rand stepped out of the shadows.

Nels hardly recognized him. The stained, dusty riding leathers he'd worn when he galloped away from them had been replaced by brilliant scarlet and blue silk over gilded chainmail, and his blonde head, bare before, now wore a silvered helmet crowned with an ornate, spread-winged eagle, repeated in silver thread on the breast of his tunic and in gold on the jewelled hilt of his sword.

Dart gaped at him. "*Prince* Rand?"

Nels stared at her. *Prince?* He looked back at Rand. His father's lessons came back to him. Only the royal household could wear the symbol of the eagle. And Athelras's son's name was . . .

Rand bowed. "At your service."

But if he was the prince, then the father he'd wanted them to meet was . . .

"King Athelras offers you his hospitality," Rand said. "You will do us great honour by accepting it."

Dart and Nels glanced at each other, dumbfounded.

Rand laughed. "I sent some messages when we reached the army. My father has prepared a great celebration. The entire populace is waiting inside to cheer you all the way to the palace. You're heroes—you saved the Heartland!"

"But I wasn't trying to save the Heartland," Nels protested. He put his good arm around Dart. "Just her."

"Which was precisely why you were able to trigger the Unicorn's power," said a new voice, and another man, wearing a black robe with a silver star picked out on its right breast, came into the sunlight.

Nels gaped. "Shadow!"

His erstwhile wagonmate bowed. "I am very glad to see you still alive," he said. "I've been berating myself for weeks for not telling you everything I knew about the Dark Unicorn when it first came to you."

Nels considered that. If he'd gone straight to Athelras with the unicorn, he wouldn't have met Dart—and as far as he was concerned, that would have been a worse disaster than the collapse of the Wall. "So tell me now," he said. "How did my desire to save Dart end up saving the whole Heartland?"

Shadow seemed relieved Nels wasn't angry. "Your outpouring of love for her at that moment, in that place, echoed the outpouring of Gondwain's love for the Heartland when he built the Wall. And somehow, after all these centuries, Gondwain's will still exerted enough power to rebuild it." He looked thoughtful. "Could Gondwain actually somehow still exist inside the Unicorn? Could it be that he—"

The Prince cut him off. "Leave the theological discussions to your Star Brethren, Shadow. Later." He grinned at Nels. "The point is, you did it, on purpose or by accident, and the people want to honour you."

"You did say *everybody* in the city is waiting to cheer us?" Dart asked suddenly.

"They'd better be. My father issued a royal decree."

"Even my 'family'?"

Rand grinned again. "I'd bet my sword on it."

Dart started forward. "Then what the blazes are we waiting for?"

Rand forestalled her with a raised hand. "For another family."

For a moment, Nels stared at him, not understanding, then suddenly saw someone else coming through the shadows of the gate. He gasped, then broke away from Dart, running to meet the sturdy, greying woman who emerged into the sunlight. "Mama!"

And then a crowd of laughing, crying, hugging people enveloped him: his sisters, his brothers, his father . . .

Dart watched silently.

But Nels, for all his joy, took only a moment to notice her absence. He turned to look for her, turned his back on his family, and went to her.

She looked down at the ground as he approached, but he cupped her chin in his hand and raised her eyes to meet his. "I have something for you," he murmured. He pulled the Dark Unicorn free from his neck and held it out to her.

She stared at it without touching it. "But . . ."

"It's nothing but a carving now," he said, "but you know what it once was. And when you look at it, you'll remember what I feel for you." He pressed it into her hand, kissed her gently, then turned and walked back to his family. He hushed their questions and glanced back at Dart, standing where he had left her, slowly turning the unicorn over and over in her hand. "Well, what the blazes are you waiting for?" he yelled.

A slow smile spread across her face, and then she ran to join him.

THE END

ABOUT EDWARD WILLETT

Edward Willett is the award-winning author (under his own name and as E.C. Blake and Lee Arthur Chane) of more than sixty books of science fiction, fantasy, and nonfiction for readers of all ages, including twelve novels for DAW Books. He has been shortlisted multiple times for Saskatchewan Book Awards, and won for his young adult fantasy *Spirit Singer* (Shadowpaw Press). He won Canada's top science fiction and fantasy award, the Aurora, for his second novel for DAW, *Marseguro,* and has been shortlisted several times since, including for his most recent young adult science fiction novel, *Star Song* (Shadowpaw Press). Ed has also won an Aurora Award for his podcast, *The Worldshapers.* In addition to being a writer and editor, Ed is a professional actor and singer. He lives in Regina, Saskatchewan, with his wife, Margaret Anne Hodges, a professional engineer.

Founded by award-winning author Edward Willett as a sister company to his traditional publishing company, Shadowpaw Press, Endless Sky Books is an author services company that assists authors with publishing all kinds of books, from children's books to poetry to novels to nonfiction. Select titles are released under the Endless Sky Books imprint.

Find out more about Endless Sky Books on our website, endless-sky-books.com, and visit our sister publisher, Shadowpaw Press, at shadowpawpress.com.

MORE BOOKS FOR YOUNG READERS

Middle-Grade Books

Stay by Katherine Lawrence

The Canadian Chills series by Arthur Slade

Fireboy by Edward Willett

Young Adult Books

The Headmasters by Mark Morton

The Sun Runners by James Bow

Tales from the Silence by James Bow

The Night Girl by James Bow

The Emir's Falcon by Matt Hughes

Blue Fire by E. C. Blake

The Ghosts of Spiritwood by Martine Noël-Maw

Star Song

Spirit Singer

From the Street to the Stars

The Shards of Excalibur Series

Soulworm

by Edward Willett

www.ingramcontent.com/pod-product-compliance
Lightning Source LLC
Chambersburg PA
CBHW031046310726
48969CB00007B/2138